LIVING IN THE DIVINE WILL

God's Greatest Gift

New Book Edition

Professionally Formatted Edition

David J. Sobnosky

Contents

Preface

Jesus Made It Clear To Luisa That He Wants This Gift Known.

Jesus Teaches Us:

Book Of Heaven – Vol. 13, Dec. 5,1921

"The Work is already done. There is nothing left except to make it known, so that, not only you, but also others may take part in these great blessings."

Message From The Author:

I Wrote This Book To Help Provide A Simple And Basic Explanation Of What This Astounding Gift Of Living In The Divine Will Is And How It Works.

Humanity Is In Desperate Need Of This New And Higher Way Of Living

As Refuge From The Chastisements Which Are Upon Us.

Epigraph

"Know that My Love is so much that I will forget about your past life,

your sins, all your evil; and I will bury them in the ocean of my Love to burn them all away;

And then we will begin a new life together, all of My Will."

(Words which Jesus gives to His children through Luisa Piccarreta, 1925)

See My Chapter: The Three Appeals

Jesus Speaking To Luisa Piccarreta

Disclaimer

Living In The Divine Will

God's Refuge For Our Time – Easily Explained

Author David J. Sobnosky

My Intent is to write everything in conformity with the Bible, The Catholic Faith, and the Writings of <u>Luisa Piccarreta.</u>

My Own Pictures Are Displayed.

I Do Not Claim That I Have Any Association With Any Quoted Sources, Or That They Are Endorsing Any Of My Writings. I have freely emphasized with my own punctuation, words, and quotes.

I have quoted from The Book Of Heaven, Kindle Edition 36 Volumes Of Luisa Piccarreta, Servant of God; Imprimatur Archbishop Giuseppe M. Leo, October 1926; Archdiocese Traini, 1928:

Alternate Title:

The Call of the Creature to the Order, the Place and the Purpose for Which He Was Created By God.

ASIN: B08YYZYM44, publication date March 14th, 2021

My Purpose Is To Point People To The Writings Of Luisa Piccarreta And The Gift Of The Divine Will For The Healing Of The Nations.

Introduction

This Is The Greatest Message About The Way God Planned Us To Be From The Beginning–

That You Will Ever Hear Because It Is From Jesus Himself To Luisa Piccarreta.

Jesus Tells Us That There Is No Message More Important!

You can search Luisa Piccarreta Book Of Heaven, Which Is The 36 Volume Message Jesus Dictated To Luisa.

My Book Explains

The Basic Message And Gift That Jesus Gave To Luisa For Her And For All Mankind,

Which Is The Greatest Gift Ever Possible From God.

Did You Ever Wonder, If Jesus Is The Messiah, Then Why Is There Still Sin And Death?

Jesus Came In The Redemption And Did It All- But Had To Prepare Humanity For His Return And To Give Us The Gift Of The Sanctification- To Be Made Holy.

This Gift Of The Divine Will Is Now Available To All People As Our Refuge In These Times Of Tribulation, And To Make Us Holy For The Era Of Peace Which Has Been Granted To The Entire Earth After The Cleansing Of The Earth-

"No More Sin And No More Death." Revelation 21:4

Jesus Is Gathering His Remnant From The Four Corners Of The Earth To Give Us The Greatest Gift That God Could Ever Give Us.

We Are The Most Blessed People To Have Ever Been Born Because This Gift Is Now Available To Us.

Father Young: "... The Divine Will Is All About The Coming Of The Kingdom Because Jesus Brings The Kingdom To Earth, The Kingdom That Was Lost."

"I Will Ask The Holy Spirit To Anoint Us Because This Is the Most Important Thing That We Can Ever Learn."

Fr. Robert Young OFM – One Of "The Originals" Divine Will Priests

From His Talk: Introduction To The Divine Will

You Tube @Romeo Hernandez

Gods Has Given The Greatest Gift Ever Possible To Humans!

We Are The Most Blessed People That Have Ever Lived

Because We Live In The Time When God Has Given

This Biblically Promised Gift

Of The Divine Will

Back To Humanity.

This Is The Greatest Gift That God Could Ever Give To Humans And He Has Given It To A Woman, Luisa Piccarreta (1865-1947), Of Corato, Italy, For Her And For All Humanity.

She is The Servant Of God, Luisa Piccarreta The Greatest Saint After Jesus And Mary, And The Greatest Prophet Of Our Time.

We Just Have To Learn About This Gift, Receive It, And Live In It.

God Knew That You And I Would Be Living Right Now, And Everything In History And Everything In Our Lives Has Prepared Us To Learn About, Receive, And Live In This Gift.

The Messiah's Mission Was To Restore The Kingdom Upon The Earth.

If Jesus Came To Earth To Restore The Kingdom, Then Why Is There Still Sin And Death?

Jesus Explained To Luisa Piccarreta The Messiah's Mission

The Messiah's Mission Was To Restore Things The Way It Was In The Garden Of Eden Before The Fall.

The Restoration Of The Kingdom Is A Two Step Process,

The Redemption And The Sanctification,

And This Ushers In The Era Of Peace For The Whole Earth.

We Received The Redemption 2,000 Years Ago By Jesus' Life, Death, And Resurrection.

But Most Christians Forget That Jesus Promised That He Would Return And Give

Humanity New Hearts And A New Spirit, And Usher In An Era Of Peace For The Entire World.

The Bridegroom Is The Church And It Would Be Made Spotless And Clean And Usher In The New Era Of Peace On The Earth.

We Were Seeking Salvation But It's A Two Step Process: Redemption Which Is Salvation And The Sanctification Which Is Perfection, To Be Made Holy.

Jesus Appeared To Luisa And Gave Her The Biblically Promised Gift Of The Sanctification, This Is Called The Gift Of The Divine Will.

The Divine Will Is The Sanctification Of Humanity And The Earth.

This Ushers In The Era Of Peace For The Entire World That The Bible Calls The Millennium Of Jesus' Reign On Earth After The Tribulation.

We Will Reign With Jesus As Kings And
Priests.

Jesus Has Now Given To Humanity The
Greatest Gift That God Can Give Creatures.

This Gift Of The Divine Will Is Rebuilding The
Church.

Jesus Explained The Times We Live In And
Gave Luisa The Greatest Gift Possible For
Humans And That We Need During These
Times.

Jesus Told Luisa That We Live In The Time Of
The Greatest Purification, As The Times Of
Noah, In Which Most Of This Generation Will Be
Destroyed But Then Comes The Great Event Of
The Era Of Peace Which Has Been Granted To
The Survivors.

God Is Restoring Human Nature To Our Original State That We Held In The Garden Of Eden.

This Is The Gift Of Living In The Divine Will That Adam And Eve Lost.

This New And Higher Way Of Living Is Our Spiritual Refuge In These Times Of The Great Tribulation.

This Is How God Is Reclaiming Humanity And The Earth From Satan And Ushering In The Era Of Peace For Entire World.

Our Times

Jesus Explained To Luisa Piccarreta

The Times In Which We Are Living, And The Problem With The Human Condition And Gave Her The Cure, For Herself And For All Humanity.

This Gift Is An Overflowing Of God's Mercy.

"Mercy Is Love In Action."

Fr. Peter Prusakiewicz

This Is God Pouring Out His Power From The Center Of The Trinity Into Those Who Receive The Divine Will And To All, To The Degree That They Are Disposed To Receive It.

See Quote God Unleashing His Power In Luisa.

This Is The Power Of God Being Unleashed From The Center Of The Trinity.

The Divine Will, We Are Talking About Here, Is God Himself.

This Is The Substance And Essence Of God That Contains All Of God.

This Is The Source And Generative And Operative Power That Runs The Trinity.

And Humans Were ORIGIONALLY Created To Have That Same Operative Power That Runs The Trinity To Live In Us, And To Run Our Lives.

In One Instant In the Divine Will You Receive All The Graces Of All the Sacraments Ever Given- And More- You Receive Union With God.

God Is Giving Away His Interior Life To Us In The Divine Will. Our Struggle Is Over - To The Degree That We Are Willing To Make the Greatest Of Sacrifices To Live In The Divine Will.

UP UNTIL NOW HUMANS HAD TO STRUGGLE TO CONFORM OUR HUMAN WILL "TO DO" GOD'S WILL-

BUT NOW IN "THE GIFT OF LIVING IN THE DIVINE WILL" THAT STRUGGLE IS OVER.

NOW WE CAN LIVE "In" GOD'S WILL, And God's Will Can Live In Us

*THIS GIFT Has Never Before Been Given To
"Fallen" Human Beings.*

*All Humans Since Adam And Eve Have Been
Conceived With Original Sin And Disconnected
From The Fullness Of The Divine Will,*

*Adam And Eve Who Were Created And Lived In
The Divine Will, Till They Sinned And That Pulled
Their Human Will Out Of The Divine Will.*

*This Changed Our Human Nature To A Fallen
State, But God Did Not Abandon Us.*

*He Left The Possibility That We Could Return To
The Original State Of Grace That Humans Were
ORIGIONALLY CREATED TO LIVE IN, WHEN GOD
DETERMINED THAT THAT TIME HAD ARRIVED.*

*AND THAT TIME HAS NOW ARRIVED ON EARTH
NOW.*

*Jesus And Mary Lived In The Divine Will All
Their Lives On Earth And Now In Heaven For
Eternity.*

But It Was Not Until JESUS APPEARED TO LUISA PICCARRETA, OF CORATO, ITALY AND GAVE HER THE GIFT OF THE DIVINE WILL FOR HER AND FOR ALL HUMANITY That This Gift Was Again Available To Humanity.

WE JUST HAVE TO LEARN ABOUT IT, RECEIVE IT, AND LIVE IN IT.

WE SIGN OURSELVES OVER TO GOD'S DIVINE WILL, AND GOD'S DIVINE WILL TAKES OVER OUR HUMAN WILL AND DIRECTS OUR LIVES COMPLETELY.

The Easiest Way To Explain The Divine Will Is That It Is A Divine Possession.

We Sign Ourselves Over To God's Divine Possession, And He Possesses Us Completely. We Call Jesus Into Doing All Our Actions – Our Acts

And we Accompany Him In All He Is Doing In Us.

This Is The Hard Part In The Beginning – To Be Constantly Faithful And Attentive.

WE LIVE IN THE DIVINE WILL AND THE DIVINE WILL LIVES IN US.

THIS IS HOW THE BLESSED SOULS LIVE IN HEAVEN.

WE ARE BEING OFFERED HEAVEN IN US – RIGHT NOW ON EARTH.

THIS IS THE FULFILLMENT OF THE OUR FATHER PRAYER, "Thy Will Be Done On Earth As It Is In Heaven."

This is The Kingdom Of God Descending to Earth In Us.

The Kingdom Of God Is A Divine Indwelling, But On God's Terms.

God Is Reclaiming Humanity

And The Earth!

If The Messiah Came To Restore The Earth To The Way It Was Before The Fall, And He Did, Then Did You Ever Wonder Why There Is Still Sin And Death?

Jesus Explained The Problem With The Human Condition To Luisa Piccarreta:

Human Beings Have Been Living In A Fallen Nature All Of Human History Since Adam And Eve.

The Human Person Living In A Fallen Sate Is Living With Their Human Will In Charge Of Their Life.

That Is Why There Is Disorder On The Earth.

And Jesus Gave Luisa Piccarreta The Cure For
Her And For All Humans Alive Right Now.

The Gift Of The Divine Will Recreates Those Who Will Receive It – In The Image And Likeness Of God–

and This Restores Humanity To The Way We Were Living Spiritually In The Garden Of Eden Before the Fall,

And This Will Be Manifest In The World – After The Purification – As the Era Of Peace.

This Is God's Light Shining In The Darkness!

And Is Arising And Overcoming The Darkness!

We Are The Most Blessed People To Have Ever Been Born Because We Are Alive When This Gift Is Available!

Jesus Tells Luisa That **It is Our Responsibility To Learn About This Gift**, and To Recognize And Heed His Voice Speaking To Luisa And To Us.

If You Will Look Into Luisa Piccarreta And The Gift Of The Divine Will That Jesus Gave To Luisa Piccarreta, There Are Ample Proofs That These Revelations Are True And This Is Jesus Speaking to Us.

Please see My Chapter: Luisa Has Been Fully Vetted [By The Catholic Church.]

This Corresponds Completely To The Bible Promises And Warnings:

Luke 18:8-9 KJV

"I tell you that he will avenge them speedily.

Nevertheless when the Son of man cometh, shall he find faith on the earth?

And he spake this parable unto certain which trusted in themselves that they were righteous, and despised others:"

John 10:27 KJV

"My Sheep hear my voice, and I know them, and they follow me."

Revelation 3:20 - KJV

"Behold, I stand at the door, and knock; If any man hear my voice, and open the door, I will come in to him, and will sup with him, and he with me."

John 17:21-23 KJV

"That they all may be one; As thou, Father, art in me, and I in thee,

that they also may be one in us; that the world may believe that thou hast sent me.

And the glory which thou gavest me I have given them; that they may be one,

even as we are one: I in them, and thou in me,

that they may be made perfect in one; and that the world may know that thou hast

sent me, and hast loved them, and thou hast loved me."

THIS GIFT Of THE DIVINE WILL

IS THE PROMISED GIFT THAT JESUS WOULD
RETURN INTO BELIEVERS

AND PREPARE HIS BRIDE– THE CHURCH TO
LIVE WITH ONE WILL

– IN AN ERA OF PEACE UPON THE EARTH.

This Is All In The Bible In Seed Form–

The Gift Of The Divine Will Is The More Detailed Explanation By Jesus Himself Of How He Is Reclaiming Humanity And Bestowing The Gifts That Adam And Eve Lost Into Us.

We Have To Be Willing To Learn About It, Receive It, And Live In It!

This Is Heaven In Us, Ahead Of Time;

This Is The Promised Restoration Of The Kingdom,

And The Sanctification Of Mankind!

I Bring You Tidings Of Great Joy (Luke 2,10)

(A Work Of Fr. Pablo Martin– Civitavecchia 1992)

Bible Quotes On The Divine Will

Jesus says, "I have food to eat that you do not know ... My food is to do the Will of Him Who sent Me and to complete His work." (John 4, 32- 34)

"We do not cease praying for you and to ask that you have a full knowledge of his Will with every knowledge and spiritual intelligence." (Col 1,9)

"...since God has made known to us the Mystery of His Will. (Eph 1,9)

(Therefore, the Divine Will is object of the most sublime knowledge and is also a mystery "hidden from eternal centuries in the mind of God." -cfr. Rom. 16,25: Eph.3, 1-5, 9-12, etc.)

"Therefore, after having prepared your mind for action, be vigilant, place every hope and that grace which will be given when Jesus Christ is revealed." (1PT. 1,13)

(The Divine Will is a 'grace', a future gift, the most desirable, bound to the future Revelations or Parousia of Christ.)

"Most dear ones, even now we are the sons of God, but that which we will be has not yet been revealed. We know then that when He will be manifested, we will be similar to Him because we will see Him as He is." (1 Jn.3,2)

(In fact, this is a Revelation that for Saint John was for the future and that regards Jesus and regards us, which will bring us back to the lost Divine Likeness.)

THE GIFT OF THE DIVINE WILL

JESUS GAVE THE GIFT OF THE DIVINE WILL

TO LUISA PICCARRETA

(1865-1947), OF CORATO, ITALY,

FOR HER AND FOR ALL OF HUMANITY.

We Are Being Raised Up To Live A New And Higher Divine Life,

And Given God's Refuge –

To Protect Us In The Purification And The Great Tribulation

That Is Upon Us,

And To Usher In The Era Of Peace

For The Entire Earth.

The Times We Live In

We Live In The Times Of The Purification

And The Great Tribulation.

It's Nature Rising Up Against Man,

Man Rising Up Against Man,

And God's Chastisements Of Fire From Heaven.

And It's All Because Man Is Out Of The Will Of God.

But God Has Given Us The Gift

That Restores Humanity

And The Earth To A Peaceful Eden.

In The Midst Of This Age Of Terror

Which Is Upon Us,

The Gift That Adam And Eve Lost

Has Now Been Given Back To Us.

This Gift Comes Through The Catholic Church

But Is For All Nations and All People

God Is Passing Out New Hearts

WE HAVE ALL BEEN WAITING FOR GOD TO GIVE US

THE BIBLICALLY PROMISED -NEW HEARTS–

AND THE FULLNESS OF THE HOLY SPIRIT-

TO USHER IN THE PROMISED MILLENNIUM OF PEACE –

THE GLORIOUS NEW ERA FOR ALL MANKIND.

GOD IS PASSING OUT NEW HEARTS-

HIS OWN DIVINE WILL.

THE DIVINE WILL IS THE DIVINE POWER

BEING POURED OUT INTO MANKIND!

THIS IS THE GIFT THAT ADAM AND EVE LOST.

JESUS AND MARY LIVED IN THE DIVINE WILL.

This Gift has never been available to Fallen Human Beings - That's Us-

Until it was given to Luisa Piccarreta For Her

And For All Humanity

(We Just Have To Learn About It, Receive It And Live In It!)

Ezekiel 36: 22-28 KJV

"A new heart also will I give you, and a new

spirit will I put within you:

and I will take away the stony heart out of your
flesh,

and I will give you an heart of flesh.

*And I will put my spirit within you, and cause you
to walk in my statutes, and ye shall keep my
judgments, and do them. And ye shall dwell in the
land that I gave to your fathers; and ye shall be my
people, and I shall be your God."*

Message For The World!

THE GIFT OF THE DIVINE WILL IS GOD

GIVING US HIS OWN BEATING HEART

FROM THE CENTER OF THE TRINITY

THIS IS THE SAME HEART THAT ALL THREE

PERSONS OF THE TRINITY SHARE

TO MAKE IT THE HEART OF EACH OF US

AND THE HEART OF THE WORLD.

THIS IS GOD'S PLAN:

WE ARE ALL RECEIVING THE SAME HEART
OF GOD

IN THE GIFT OF THE DIVINE WILL

AND WE WILL ALL LIVE

A NEW AND HIGHER DIVINE LIFE –

IN HARMONY

IN THE ERA OF PEACE.

Quote From The Book Of Heaven– Volume 17–
October 6, 1924

How the Divine Will is primary heartbeat of the soul and all created things

Luisa Speaking:

"I was fusing myself in the Holy Divine Will, and My Sweet Jesus, moving in My Interior, told me:

"My daughter, how beautiful it is to see a soul fusing herself in My Will!

As she fuses herself in it, <u>the created heartbeat takes its place in life in the Uncreated Heartbeat, and forms a single one, running and beating together with the Uncreated Heartbeat.</u>

<u>This is the greatest happiness of the human heart: to palpitate in the Eternal Heartbeat Of Its Creator.</u>

My will makes it fly, and the human heartbeat flings <u>itself into the center of its Creator."</u>

"Then I said to him: tell me, my love, how many times does your will go around through all creatures?

And Jesus: "My daughter, in each heartbeat of creature my Will forms Its complete round through all of Creation.

And just as the heartbeat in the creature is continuous, and if the heartbeat ceases life ceases, in order to give Divine Life to all creatures, <u>My Will, more than heartbeat, goes around and forms the Heartbeat of My Will in every heart.</u>

See then how My Will is in every creature, as primary heartbeat because her own is secondary: and if I feel any heartbeat of creature, it is by virtue of the heartbeat of my Will."

"Even more, my Will forms in her two heartbeats:

one for the human heart, as life of the body,

and one for the soul, as heartbeat and life of the soul.

But do you want to know what this heartbeat of my Will does in the creature?

If she thinks, my will runs and circulates like blood in the veins of the soul and gives her The Divine Thought that she may put aside the human thought and give place to the word of the Will. If she works, if she walks, if she loves, my Will wants the place of her work, of her step, of her love....

In Sum, in everything, My Will has Its Life, and with its Power, it forms the Act it Wants.

So it maintains harmony in all created things informs in them the different effects, colors, offices of which each of them contains.

Therefore, I recommend that you never go out of my will, if you do not want to multiply my sorrow, and lose the purpose for which you were created.

This Gift Is Divine Life.”

THE KINGDOM WAS FORMED IN MARY, AND NOW IN US.

Book of Heaven – V19 – 6.20.26

"...if I came in Redemption, I came to realize My Ideal and My Primary Purpose– that is, the Kingdom of My Will in souls.

This is so True, that in order to come, I formed *My First Kingdom of the Supreme Volition* in the Heart of My Immaculate Mamma– outside of My Kingdom I would never have come upon the earth."

JESUS IS SHARING MARY'S HEART WITH HUMANITY

The Sun Of My Will, Vatican Released Biography Of Luisa Piccarreta

P. 227,

"Dying on the cross, Jesus wanted His Mother to become mother of all people, and He wanted that she do for all creatures what she did for Him.

Therefore, her maternity extends to all the acts of all people, so that Jesus may see them all protected and tucked away in her maternal love.

So, just as His inseparable Momma extended her maternity inside and outside of Jesus' humanity, God established her and confirmed her as Mother of every creature's thought, breath, heartbeat, and word.

In the end, Jesus will share His place in Mary's maternal heart with whoever decides to live in His Divine Will."

Book Of Heaven – Volume 36

December 28, 1938

The Maternity Of The Queen Of Heaven

Jesus Speaking:

"I will surrender My place to one who lives in my Volition in Her Maternal Heart.

She will raise them in Me, will guide their steps, will hide them in Her Maternity and Sanctity; one will see impressed in all their acts Her Maternal Love and Her Sanctity;

They will be Her true children, that will resemble Me in everything".

THIS GIFT OF LIVING IN THE DIVINE WILL

– THAT JESUS GAVE TO LUISA PICCARRETA

(1865–1947) OF CORATO, ITALY

This Comes Through The Catholic Church But Is For Everyone.

Jesus Told Luisa That The Greatest Sign That The Era Of Peace Is Coming Is That This Gift Has Been Given.

Book Of Heaven −Volume 15− July 14, 1923

The Paternal Goodness Wants To Open Another Era Of Grace

Jesus to Luisa:

"**The world is exactly at the same stage when I was about to come upon earth.**

All were awaiting a great event, a New Era; as it indeed occurred.

<u>**The same now; Since the great Event is coming- the New Era in which the Will of God will be done on earth as it is in Heaven-**</u> everyone is waiting for this new Era, being tired of the present one, but not knowing what this novelty, this change is, just as they did not know it when I came upon the earth.

This wait is a sure sign that the hour is near.

<u>*But the most certain sign is that I am manifesting what I want to do;*</u>

<u>*And turning to a soul, just as I turned to my Mama in descending from Heaven to earth, I communicate to her My Will and the goods and effects it contains, in order to give It as Gift to all humanity.*</u>"

What's New is that We Can Now Sign Ourselves Over

To God's Divine Will, Which Is His Divine Heart –

And With Our Cooperation, His Will Takes Over Direction Of Our Human Will, And Thus Our Life.

(His Heart is His Will.)

Thus, All Those Who Live In This Gift

Are All Living With The Same Heart –

Which is God's Heart And His Will

and We All Live In Perfect Harmony In The Era Of Peace.

The Problem With The Human Condition

Jesus Appeared To Servant Of God Luisa Piccarreta And Explained The Problem With The Human Condition

and Gave Her The Cure For Her And For All Humanity.

The Problem Is That We Are Living In

'A Fallen Nature' In Which Our Human Will

Is In Control Of Our Lives "On Its Own."

This Fallen Nature Has Been The Way All Human Beings Have Been Living

All Of Human History Since Our First Parents.

(Except Jesus And Mary Who Lived All Their Lives In The Divine Will– And Luisa Piccarreta Who Was Given This Gift For Her And For All Who Come After Her– Who Will Learn About It, Receive It, And Live In It.)

The Problem:

Our Human Will Is Running Our Lives, 'On It's Own

But Our Human Will Was Never Meant To Run Our Lives– 'On It's Own'

– The Human Will 'On It's Own'– Cut Off From The Operating Life Of The Divine Will – Is Selfish And Egotistic And Erratic And Defective.

This Is The Only Problem With The Human Condition.

We were never meant to live separate from God's Divine Will.

We may not realize it, but everything we do has a selfish element.

We are all our own "lttle gods," all fighting each
other for control.

The Solution:

*We Sign Ourselves Back Over To God's
Divine Will– Running Our Human Will
And Directing Our Lives.*

God Recreates Us In The Image And Likeness Of
God The Way We Were Meant To Live From The
Beginning.

*Jesus Dictated "The Book Of Heaven" To Luisa
Piccarreta Which Is Our Instruction Guide To Live In
The Divine Will.*

We pass through Purgatory ahead of time. We
are Cleansed and Live in Heaven and on Earth at
the same time.

It's An All-New Life - All Happiness!

THIS IS A NEW AND HIGHER WAY TO LIVE THAT WE CAN ALL ENTER INTO.

"THIS GIFT IS DIVINE LIFE"

We Take On This Gift Of Divine Life And Live In It In Everything We Do.

(See Chapter: **Two Generations:**)

Book Of Heaven – Volume 14 – October 27, 1922

Inheritance Of Jesus For The Creatures. Two Generations.

Jesus To Luisa:

"Even more, you must know that my Humanity contained two generations within itself: the children of darkness and the children of light.

I came to rescue the former, and so I gave out my Blood in order to save them. My Humanity was holy, and nothing did It inherit of <u>the miseries of the first man;</u> and although it was similar in natural features, it was untouchable to the slightest spot which could shade my sanctity.

My only inheritance was the Will of my Father, in which I was to carry out all of my human acts, to form in me ***the generation of <u>the children of light</u>."***

This Gift Is Ushering In The Era Of Peace For The Entire World.

We can all share the same Divine Heart Of God Which Will Direct All Our Lives. This Directs All Our Activities And Solves All Human Problems.

(We Just Have To Learn About It, Sign Our-self Over To It, And Live In It.)

Book Of Heaven

Vol. 13 – Dec. 5, 1921

Jesus To Luisa:

"The work is already done. There is nothing left except to make it known, so that, not only you, but also others may take part in these Great Blessings."

This Is The Biblically Promised Sanctification Of Humanity In Which Satan Is Chained And Vanquished For 1,000 Years.

We Will All Have The Same Heart: Jesus, Mary, And Luisa And Now All Those Who Have Come After Luisa And Have Said Yes To This Gift - All Live In Union With God's Own Heart.

This Is The Gift That Adam And Eve Lost That Has Now Been Given Back To Humanity.

THE ONLY QUESTION IS WILL YOU PARTICIPATE IN THIS GIFT AND THE ERA OF PEACE?

The Knowledge Is Critical

There Is Divine Power In Every Word Of *The Book Of Heaven*,

If You Don't Know What This Gift Is, Then You Cannot Desire It, Or Sign Yourself Over To It, Or Live In It.

THE NITTY GRITTY

Jesus Told Luisa That He Always Meant The Sanctification To Be Simple And Easy To Do,

And It, Is If We Are Willing to Make The Greatest Of Sacrifices And Sign Over Our Human Will To God's Divine Will In All Things.

We Don't Lose Our Free Will, Ever. God Must Have The Complete Free Consent Of Our Will To

Live This Way- The Way The Blessed Live In Heaven.

We Give The Complete Free Consent Of Our Will For Eternity.

Our Free Will Is Activated- Our Free Will Must Desire This Gift And Give Our Fiat Now For All Eternity.

We Do Lose All Our Rights, We Sign Them Over to God.

God Knows What Is Best, And This Is Total Freedom For Us And For This Good God - To Make Us Happy Beyond Our Wildest Imaginations.

The Sun Of My Will
Luisa Piccarreta, p.222

"...Mary says, "May it be done to me" *(Lk 1:38)*, and Jesus says," Not my will but yours be done"

(*Lk 22:42*), and Luisa encounters the same situation.

It is not she who wants "to do" the Will of the Father, but it is the Father – who by "fusing" their two wills- has Luisa's life in His hands.

She will have to make it understood that God is not a master to obey; rather He is someone who wants humanity to be fully realized- *and that can only happen when the individual freely wants the Will of God.*

...P. 223

What is new is the continuous exchange *between the Divine Will, that's restoring the divine likeness that was lost through sin.* Through the gift of His Will to the individual, God forms "His life" in the person, *His way of "real presence."*

Therefore this person serves as "another humanity" for Him, as Carmelite Sister Elizabeth of the Trinity would say. Obviously, this is not some kind of "hypostatic union" (the union of

27

divine and human natures and one person), *but is the union of two wills – the human and divine– united in one act of willing, like two hearts beating in unison.*

That way this individual becomes the triumph of Jesus; it is "another Jesus," not by nature, but by the gift of grace according to the words of St. John, "because as He is, so are we in this world" *(1 Jn 4: 17).*

The Era Of Divine Will

We Live In the Era Of The Divine Will Which began on September 8, 1889 when Luisa Piccarreta Received The Gift Of The Divine Will for Her And For All Humanity, Which Will Culminate In The Era Of Peace After The Chastisements.

The Living In The Divine Will Is The Middle- Silent Coming Of Jesus To Earth- In His Mystical Body - The Faithful Members Of His Church.

This Is The Fulfillment Of The Our Father Prayer:

"Thy Kingdom come, Thy Will be done in Earth, as it is in Heaven."

(Mathew 6:10 KJV)

We humans are that Earth.

This Is The Most Blessed Time For Human Beings To Be Alive! – If We Learn About This GIFT, Receive It, And Live In It!

This Is The Era In Human History When The Gift Of The Living In The Divine Will That Adam And Eve Lost Has Been Given Back To Humanity.

It Has All Come Together In Our Time.

All that has been done in Heaven and on Earth has been prelude to God giving us this Gift,

To make it accessible to us and to prepare us to receive it.

Follow The Miracles Of Jesus And The Apostles. Look To The Church And The Sacraments, The Bible, The Lives and Writings Of The Catholic Saints, And All The Apparitions Of Jesus And Our Lady: They All Lead To Luisa Piccarreta, And This Gift.

Over The Centuries, God has allowed printing presses, and the industrial revolution, with factories, and cars and washing machines to free up our time; and education so that the masses can read, and computers and technology and the internet so that we can learn about The Divine Will.

If You Will Look Into Luisa Piccarreta And The Gift Of The Divine Will That Jesus Gave To Luisa Piccarreta, There Are Ample Proofs That This is True And It Is Jesus Speaking to Us.

Please see My Chapter: Luisa Has Been Fully Vetted [By The Catholic Church.]

Jesus Tells Luisa That It is Our Responsibility To Learn About This Gift, and To Recognize And Heed His Voice Speaking To Luisa And To Us.

We Are Choosing Heaven Or Hell Right Now.

The Sanctification Of Humanity

This Living In The Divine Will is The Sanctification Of Humanity,

And It Is The Same As The Redemption,

In That,

It Is Our Responsibility To Seek It, Learn about It And Live In It.

Our Life On Earth And Our Eternity Depends On It.

This Is The Time Of Decision.

This Gift Is God's Refuge That We Must Enter In

For Our Protection And Our Sanctification,

For This Time Of Chastisement That Has Begun.

On The Outside Is The Gnashing Of Teeth.

I Bring You Tidings Of Great Joy Selection of Passages about the Divine Will – (A work of Fr. Pablo Martin, Civitavecchia1992)

(33)   Book Of Heaven – Vol. 36 – September 18, 1938

God resorts to every means so that His Will might triumph.

Jesus to Luisa;

"...We will continue what we have been doing; we do what is needed on our part so that nothing lacks of help, of light, of good, of surprising truths so that My Will be known and reign. I will use every means of love, of graces, of chastisements; **I will touch creatures from all sides in order to make My Will reign.** And when it seems as if true good must die, it will rise up more beautiful and majestic."

Why Now

Luisa Asked Jesus Why Didn't You Give Humanity Back The Gift of The Divine Will When You Were On the Earth 2,000 Years Ago?

Jesus told Luisa That People Were Not Prepared To Receive This Gift.

The Full Gift Of What Jesus Won On The Cross Is:

The Redemption And The Sanctification.

Jesus Only Gave Us The Gifts Of The Redemption, Which Is Salvation.

This Divine Will Gift is The Biblically Promised Sanctification Of Mankind.

Jesus Paid The Full Price – But We Could Only Receive The Gifts Of The Redemption, because

Mankind was not ready to receive The Gift Of The Sanctification.

Jesus Told Luisa That Humanity First Had To Receive The Lesser Gifts To Prepare Us For The Greater Gifts.

The Divine Will Was First In Intention But Only Second In Execution.

Now We Are All Prepared To Receive The Gift Of The Divine Will – Which Is The Sanctification.

My Gift

I Believe That My Personal Gift Is That: I Can Explain The Basics Of The Divine Will and The Times That We Live In- In Easily Understandable Terms - For Common People As Well As Theologians.

As For This Author, The Divine Will Has Become My Life, and I Hope To Share Some Basic Concepts To Give You A Small Boost Up, Dear Reader.

Some Modern Readers Have No Historical Or Spiritual Background To Understand What They Are Reading In Context.

Most People Do Not Have the Time Or The Inclination To Spend Hours and Hours Reading About And Studying History and Different Religions, And Especially The Bible, The Lives And Writings Of The Catholic Saints, Apparitions Of

The Blessed Virgin Mary, And The Writings Of Luisa.

All Of Human History Is God's Revelation To Mankind, And It All Builds Up To God Giving Us Back The Gift Of the Divine Will.

The Divine Will Is God Himself and Is An Inexhaustible Fount Of Knowledge And Life- And We Will Continue To Learn About The Divine Will For Eternity In Heaven.

Chastisement

Our Times

This Is A Purification That We Are In. It Is Also Called A Chastisement – And The 7 Year Great Tribulation Is A Part Of It.

Jesus Told Luisa That This is The Only Way God Can Turn Us Humans Around – With Chastisements– And To Give Us Great Gifts To Draw Us Into Living A Renewed Existence.

Purification: the removal of impure elements...

Chastisement: a Strong Rebuke Or Punishment.

Jesus Tells Us That Most Of This Civilization And Humanity Is Being Destroyed.

This Purification Is Falling On The Good And The Evil. For Those That Die, The Good Are Going To Heaven, The Evil Are Going To Hell.

The Survivors Will Be Few, But Then We Will Live In A Renewed Existence In The Era Of Peace, Which is the Biblical Millennium Of Peace Granted To The Entire World.

THIS IS THE GREATEST TIME TO HAVE EVER BEEN ALIVE ON EARTH.

Yes, We Live At The Time Of The Greatest Chastisement That The World Has Ever Known, But We have Been Given The Greatest Spiritual Gift, The Gift OF Living In The Divine Will, As Our Refuge, Our Consolation, And Our Sanctification.

IT'S A PURIFICATION, THE GREAT TRIBULATION, AND MULTIPLE CHASTISEMENTS.

JESUS EXPLAINS THE TIMES:

Book Of Heaven

Volume 12 - January 29, 1919

Jesus To Luisa:

"My beloved daughter, I want you to know the order of my Providence. In every 2,000-year period I have renewed the world.

In the first period I renewed it with the Flood. In the second 2,000 years, I renewed it with my **coming to the earth** and manifesting my Humanity from which, as so many channels of light, my Divinity shone. <u>Now in this third renovation, after the purging of the earth and the destruction of a large part of the present generation, I will be still more generous with creatures.</u>"

(For Full Quote, SEE The Section: Jesus Explains The Times)

Our Refuge

Promises of Refuge For Those Living In The Divine Will

Four very important truths of the coming chastisements:

No 1. The Large majority of humanity shall be gone after the Chastisements:

No. 2. The Blessed Mother shall Mark all her little children of the Divine Will and they shall not be harmed by the Chastisements:

No. 3. The Chastisements shall have little or no effect upon the little children of the Divine Will:

No. 4. The Survivors of the Chastisements shall be the little children of the Holy Divine Will:

Promises of Refuge For Those Living In The Divine Will Quoted From: Divinewill.org

No 1.

The Large majority of humanity shall be gone after the Chastisements:

Book Of Heaven - Volume 2 – October 4, 1899

Jesus To Luisa: "My daughter, man is a product of the Divine Being, and since Our food is love, always reciprocal, alike and constant among the Three Divine Persons, since he came out of Our hands and from pure and disinterested love, he is like a particle of Our food.

Now, this particle has become bitter for Us; not only this, but the majority of them, by moving away from Us, have made themselves pasture for the infernal flames and food for the implacable hatred of demons, Our implacable enemies and theirs.

This is the Main Cause of Our sorrow in the loss of souls: they are Ours – they are something that belongs to Us.

Likewise, the cause that pushes Me to chastise them is the Great Love that I have for them, so as to place their souls in Safety.

"Book Of Heaven - Volume 12 – January 29, 1919:

"… My beloved daughter, I want to make known to you the order of My Providence.

"**Every Two Thousand Years I Have Renewed The World.**"

"**In The First Two Thousand Years I renewed it with the Deluge;**

In The Second Two Thousand Years I renewed it with my coming upon earth when I manifested My Humanity, from **which, as if from many fissures, My Divinity shone forth.** The good ones

44

and the very saints of the following two thousand years have lived from the fruits of My humanity and, in drops, they have enjoyed My Divinity."

"Now we are around the third 2,000 years, and there shall be a third renewal. This is the reason for the general confusion: it is nothing other than the preparation for The Third Renewal.

If in the second renewal I manifested what My Humanity did and suffered, and very little of what my Divinity was operating, *now, in this third renewal, after the earth will be purged and a great part of the current generation destroyed, I shall be even more generous with creatures,"*

(For This Full Quote See Chapter: Jesus Explains The Times)

No. 2.

The Blessed Mother shall Mark all her little children of the Divine Will and they shall not be harmed by the Chastisements:

Book Of Heaven

Volume 33 – June 6, 1935 –

"You Must Know that I always Love My children, My Beloved creatures. I would eviscerate Myself in order to not see them stricken, so Much So that in the mournful times that shall come, I have placed them all into the hands of My Celestial Mama. I have entrusted them to Her, so that She keeps them secure for Me under Her mantle.

I shall give to Her all those that She shall want, death itself shall not have power over these who shall be in the custody of My Mama."

Now while He said this, my dear Jesus made me see with deeds that The Sovereign Queen descended from Heaven with an indescribable

Majesty and a Tenderness all Maternal, and She went around in the midst of creatures in all the nations and *She Marked Her dear children, and those who Must Not be touched by the scourges."*

No. 3.

The Chastisements shall have little or no effect upon the little children of the Divine Will:

Volume 33– June 6, 1935–

"...Each one My Celestial Mama touched, the scourges had no power to touch those creatures.

Sweet Jesus gave the right to His Mama of placing in safety whomever She pleased. How moving it was to see the Celestial Empress making Her Round through all the parts of the world, that She took them in Her Maternal Hands, *She entrusted them to Her bosom, she hid them under Her Mantle, so that no evil could harm those whom her maternal goodness kept in Her custody, guarded, and defended.*

O! If everyone could see with how Much Love and Tenderness the Celestial Queen did this Office, they would cry from consolation, and they would Love She who loves them so much."

No. 4.

The Survivors of the Chastisements shall be the little children of the Holy Divine Will:

Book Of Heaven –

Volume 36 – October 2, 1938

"Daughter, I wanted to do this, by winning man through My Love, but human perfidy does not allow Me.

Therefore I shall use Justice. I shall sweep the earth, I shall take away all the harmful creatures who like poison plants, poison the innocent plants.

Once I have purified everything, My Truths shall find the way to Give to the Survivors the Life, the Balm, and the Peace that They contain; and everybody shall receive Them, <u>Giving Them the kiss of Peace, to the confusion of those who did not believe in Them and even condemned Them.</u>

My Truths shall Reign and I shall have My Kingdom on earth; My Will be done on earth as it is in Heaven.

Therefore once again, let's not move in anything. Let's do Our Way and We shall sing victory; They can do their way, in which they shall find confusion and shame of themselves.

It shall happen to them as to the blind, who don't believe in the light of the sun because they don't see it: <u>they shall remain in their blindness, while those who See It shall Enjoy and Show Off the Goods of the Light with Complete Happiness.</u>" *Fiat!*

All Of History

All Of Human History is Prelude

To God Giving The Gift of The Divine Will Back to Humans.

All Of The Old Testament Times And The Redemption Has Been To Prepare Humans To Learn About And Receive This Gift.

With This Gift, We Are Raised Up To A Higher Divine Life –

The Way We Were Meant To Live From The Beginning, Or We Will Be On The Outside Gnashing Our Teeth As We Come Into The Great Tribulation.

God Has Not Abandoned Us, And He Has Given Us - The Greatest Gift That He Could Ever Give Us- Even In Heaven- For Right Now On Earth.

The Gift Of The Divine Will Is "The Third Fiat": "The Sanctification", Which Ushers Us Into The Era Of Peace For The Whole World.

It Is Only At The End Of The Biblically Promised Millennium Of Peace- The Era Of Peace –

That Satan Will Be Released For a Short Time, then Jesus Is Coming In The Flesh For The Final Judgement –

This is The Definitive "Second Coming Of Jesus" – and Then It Is Heaven Or Hell For Everyone – For Eternity.

The "Empire Of Darkness"

The "Empire Of Darkness" Started Out

In The Mists Of The Garden Of Eden, When Adam And Eve Sinned.

This is Precisely When Satan Was Able To Infiltrate Into Our Human Condition And Became The Ruler Of The World.

We Are Part of This "Generation Of Darkness" Which Is Dying Out As Our Civilization Crumbles And The World Is Thrown Into Chaos.

We Are The Witnesses To The Fall Of This 6,000-YEAR Civilization Of Satan And The Rise Of A New Generation Of Light And The Era Of Peace Which Has Been Granted For The Entire World.

"The Empire Of Darkness" Is The Longest And Saddest Epic In History Lasting From The Fall of

Adam And Eve Until It's Last Vestiges – Which We Are Now Witnessing-

We Live In The Greatest Transition

From Not Just One Era- Which is 2,000 Years,

But From One Age To Another and Into A More Glorious Age-

The Era Of Peace.

Our Civilization Is Dying Out.

Our Fallen Human Nature Is Failing Us'

God Has Given Us A New And Divine Way Of Living

To Replace Our Fallen Nature.

The Only Question

The Only Question Is: Will You Learn About This Gift And Participate In Being Transformed Into Part Of "The New Generation Of Light" That God Is Raising Up.

Our Very Nature And Our Civilization Has Been Turned Against Us–

Nature Is Out Of Balance And Attacking Man And This Godless Civilization –

We See The Rise Of Diseases, Earthquakes, Volcanoes, Hurricanes and Floods. We See Natural Catastrophes All Lining Up On The Horizon,

But Most Of All We See The Unhappiness Of The Human Will Separated From God And Running Out Of Energy.

Some People Are Gnashing Their Teeth In Utter Frustration, While Others Are Being Surprised By The Mercy Of God Giving Himself In The Divine Will.

The Fall Of "The Empire Of Darkness"

Is What We See And Smell All Around Us. The Smell Of Marijuana Lingering In Wasted City Streets Littered With The Homeless and Hopeless.

Satan Seems To Be Powerful- And Looks To Be Large- But Is Inflated Like A Huge Parade Clown Balloon- And Is Imploding!

Man Is Out Of Energy Because He Is Out Of God's Will —

But The Most Telling Sign Of The Sad Ending Of This Civilization Is:

The Apathy Of The Most Comfortable People On Earth.

Most People Are All Wrapped Up In Their Own Problems And Concerns, <u>And Don't Want To Know What God Is Offering Us.</u>

"Then Jesus said to his disciples, truly I tell you, it will be hard for a rich person to enter the Kingdom of Heaven. Again I tell you, it is easier for a camel to go through the eye of a needle than for someone who is rich to enter the Kingdom of God."

(Mathew 19: 23-24 – NRSV)

Humans Must Be Prepared To Spend The Two Coins

That Each Of Us Is Given In Our Life,

That Is, Our Time And Our Attention,

To Learn About Jesus Appearing To Luisa Piccarreta (1865-1947) Of Corato, Italy,

And To Recognize That This Is Really That Same Jesus Who Died On The Cross Who Is Speaking To Luisa And Us.

The Living in The Divine Will Is Normal For A Human Being.

Adam And Eve Lived The Normal Human Living Before The Fall-

Walking With Jesus In Intimacy In The Cool Evening-

This Is Our Birthright And Our Heritage That we Must Reclaim.

Jesus Speaks Of Adam
Book Of Heaven –

Volume 21 - March 19, 1927

How In Creation God gave the rights to possess the Kingdom of the Divine Will.

Luisa: "I was, as usual, following the acts of the Supreme Volition in creation, and reaching the moment when God put forth the creation of man,

I united myself with the first perfect acts which Adam did when he was created, to begin with him and follow him-

57

to when he finished loving Him [God] and adoring Him [God], to when he sinned,

[to do my acts] <u>with that perfection with which he began with when he was in that unity of the Supreme Fiat.</u>

But while I was doing this, I thought to myself: "But do we have the right to this Kingdom of the Divine Volition?"

And my sweet Jesus, moving in my interior, said to me: "My daughter, you must know that before he sinned, Adam did his acts in the Divine Fiat.

This means that the Trinity had given him the possession of this Kingdom, because he was able to possess a Kingdom there must be one who forms it, one who gives it, and one who receives it.

The Divinity formed it and gave it to man, and he received it.

Adam in The First Period of Creation, possessed this Kingdom together with the Supreme Fiat, <u>*and because he was the head of all human generations, all creatures received this right of possession.*</u>

And Adam, withdrawing from our will, lost the possession of this Kingdom because by doing his own will he placed himself in a state of war with the Eternal Fiat.

...All of that did not take away the rights of his descendants to possibly once again take over the Kingdom of My Will."

Who is Luisa?

Excerpt From: Luisa Piccarreta By Bernardino Giuseppe Bucci

The Servant of God Luisa Piccarreta was born in Corato in the province of Bari, on April 23, 1865, and died there in the odor of sanctity on March 4, 1947. ... Luisa was born on the Sunday after Easter and baptized that same day.

... **Divine Providence led the little girl down paths so mysterious that she knew no joys other than God and his grace.**

One day, in fact, the Lord said to her: "I went round the earth over and over again; I looked at all creatures, one by one, in order to find the littlest of all. Among many I found you – the littlest of all. I liked your littleness and I chose you. I entrusted you to my Angels, so that they might keep you, not to make you great, but to preserve your littleness;

and now I want to begin the Great Work of the Fulfillment of My Will. Nor will you feel greater because of this; on the contrary, My Will shall make you smaller, and you shall continue to be the little daughter of your Jesus - the little daughter of My Will." (cf. Book Of Heaven - Volume XII, March 23, 192)

Excerpt From: I Bring You Tidings Of Great Joy (Luke 2,10) A Book By Fr. Pablo Martin (Civitavecchia 1992) Selection of passages about the Divine Will taken from the writings of Luisa Piccarreta, "The Little Daughter of the Divine Will."

Translators Preface This little book is the result of Fr. Pablo Martin's heartfelt response to the appeal of the Divine King for his beloved children to enter into the Reign of the Divine Will on earth as it reigns in Heaven.

Fr. Pablo is a humble, parish priest residing in Civitavecchia, Italy. He is a native of Spain and dedicated himself to the religious life upon entering a minor seminary at the age of 13. For more than 20 years Fr. Pablo has applied himself to the study of the writings of the Servant of God, Luisa Piccarreta; and in this little book he introduces us to various passages taken from her writings.

These writing of Luisa, who wrote them wholly under obedience to the confessors assigned to her by her Bishop, seems to be totally unprecedented in the history of mankind.

In them one will discover secrets of God about His Divine Will never before made known, although rooted in Sacred Scripture.

These secrets apply especially to our own times, the antecedent to the coming of The New Era of the Reign of the Divine Will prayed for by Jesus.

In that prayer He taught us to pray: "Our Father who art in Heaven hallowed be thy name:

thy Kingdom come: thy Will be done on earth as it is in Heaven..."

It is the fervent wish of the translator that those who read this little book will be moved in the depths of their souls to consecrate their human wills to God in exchange for the Gift of the Divine Will.

This is also the ardent wish of Luisa Piccarreta (1865 to 1947) whom Jesus called "the little daughter of the Divine Will."

Luisa was a voluntary victim soul whom Our Lord confined to bed in Corato, Italy for 64 years without food or water and scarcely any sleep, as he wanted her totally set aside for **her mission of heralding** the **Reign of the Divine Will on earth as in Heaven.**

To this end Jesus made known to Luisa 36 volumes, which she put into writing for the Glory of God, and for the supreme benefit of mankind.

From a relic card of Luisa:

The Servant of God Luisa Piccarreta Dominican Tertiary who died in the odor of Sanctity at Corato, (Bari) Italy on March 4th, 1947 by Padre Bernardino Guiseppe Bucci, O.F.M. Permission granted for printing: Trani, November 28, 1948 Fr. Reginaldo Addazi O.P. Archbishop.

The Servant of God, Luisa Piccarreta, Dominican Tertiary, was born at Corato, Province of Bari, Italy, on April 23rd 1865. Elect soul, seraphic spouse of Christ, humble, pious and endowed by God with extraordinary gifts;

Herald of The Kingdom of the Divine Will, true and innocent victim, and therefore effective and continuous lightning rod for Divine Justice, aroused by the indignation by the sins of mankind.

A young girl barely 18 years old (Vision or dream? To Ecclesiastical Authority the judgement.) she saw Jesus, bent under the Cross, who told her, "Soul help me!" Thereafter that solitary soul lived in continuous union with the ineffable sufferings of her Divine Spouse. From her 13th to 18th year, her angelic life was spent among outpourings of divine love and celestial favors, as well as among extraordinary signs of supernatural life.

In her 62 years of being bed-ridden she endured her hard and painful infirmity with heroic Christian strength and from her bed of pain she was the comfort of the weak and suffering souls, the light of all those who approached her for advice."

She called herself "The Little Daughter of The Divine Will," to everyone and continuously she spoke about The Divine Will, how to operate and live in it, how it is the only and sure means in order to obtain one's sanctification." ...

What Books Did Luisa Write?

Luisa Piccarreta Official Website

en.luisapiccarretaofficial.org
luisapiccarreta.com
book of heaven.com

Luisa's Magnum Opus Is The 36 Volume:

The Book Of Heaven

"The Call To The Creature To Return To the Order,

To the Place,

And to the Purpose for which it was Created By God."

This Is The Full Title Jesus Gave The Writings Of

Her 36 Volumes, Or Notebooks All Dictated By Jesus Christ,

Plus Two Other Important Books:
<u>The Passion Of Our Lord</u>, and
<u>The Blessed Virgin In The Divine Will</u>,
And Numerous Letters.

The Book Of Heaven

Everything Luisa Wrote, Jesus Was Writing In Her Writing. So It Is Said That Jesus "Dictated" All Her Works.

Luisa Wrote 36 Notebooks, Which Are Called The Book Of Heaven

The Book Of Heaven Explains The Basics Of How Our Human Will Operates in Our Life and How Living In The Divine Will Makes Us Happy And Complete.

Also The Book Of Heaven Explains The Basic Disorder Of The Human Condition - Our Fallen

Nature - Which Is Responsible For The Rise And Fall Of Civilizations, And Why People Are Not Loving God And Each Other.

The Reason Is That Humans Are Living In A Defective- Fallen Condition Disconnected From The Fullness Of The Divine Will.

Book Of Heaven – Volume 17- September 17, 1924

"... Do you see what it means to do acts in my Will? This is to live in my Will: the Sun of my Will, transforming the human will into Sun, acts in it as if in Its own center."

Afterwards, my sweet Jesus gathered all the books written by me on His Divine Will; He united them together, then He pressed them to His Heart, and with unspeakable tenderness, added: "I bless these writings from the heart. I bless every word; I bless the effects and the value they contain. These writings are part of Myself."

Luisa's Other Two Monumental Books:
<u>The Passion Of Our Lord</u>
<u>The Blessed Virgin In The Divine Will</u>

<u>The Passion Of Our Lord</u>
from website: luisapiccarreta.com

...When Luisa had finished writing The Hours Of The Passion, she wrote a letter which she gave to Saint Annibale (Di Francia) together with the book, who included it in the book's preface when he published it. From this letter, we come to appreciate how pleased Jesus is, and how many benefits are lavished upon the soul, when it practices these hours on a daily basis, as bread without which one cannot live.

Here is the letter. "... Jesus' Joy is so immense when someone meditates on The Hours Of The Passion, that he would like to see at least one copy of these meditations being used in every city and town. Because then it would be as if Jesus was hearing His Own Voice and His own Prayers which He raised to His Father during the 24 hours of His Painful Passion. *And if this is done at least by a few souls in each town and city, He Himself promises that the Divine Justice will be appeased in part, and punishments will be lessened.*

It happened that on one occasion, Saint Annibale Di Francia went to Luisa's house and recounted what had taken place on one of his visits with the Pope (being an intimate friend of Pope St. Pius X), he was frequently received by him. While with him, he wanted to introduce him to the book, The Hours Of The Passion Of Our Lord Jesus Christ, which he had been spreading. So St. Annibale read a few pages of it to the Pope specifically from The Hour Of The Crucifixion.

At a certain point, the Pope interrupted him, saying: *"Father, this book should be read while kneeling. It is Jesus Christ who is speaking."*

Words Of Jesus: "... These Hours are the most precious of all. Because they are nothing other than the repetition of what I did in the course of my mortal Life, and what I continue to do in the Most Blessed Sacrament.

The Other Monumental Work Of Luisa Is: The Virgin Mary In The Kingdom Of The Divine Will.

"Each Day For Several Weeks in the late 1920's, the Virgin Mary came from Heaven to sit at the foot of Luisa's bed and teach her the lessons contained in this book." p.1,

Here Are Mary's Own Words Telling Us About This Book:

"I come from Heaven and inviting you to enter into the Kingdom of your Mother, that is, into the Kingdom of the Divine Will. I am knocking at the door of your heart because I want you to open it to Me.

Do you realize that it is with my own hands that I'm bringing you this book as a Gift?

I am offering it to you with a mother's care so that you, and your turn upon reading it, will learn to live the way of Heaven and no longer that of earth. This Book is of gold, my child.

It will become your spiritual fortune and your happiness even here while you are on earth. In it you will find the fountain of all goods. If you are weak, you will acquire strength; If you are tempted you will conquer the temptations that come to you; If you have fallen into sin, you will feel a powerful and compassionate hand to lift you up. If you are afflicted, you will find comfort; And if you are cold, you will be given the sure means to warm yourself; if you become hungry, you will taste the exquisite food of the Divine Will, and with it nothing will ever be lacking to you.

You will never be alone because your Mother will be your sweet companion; and with every maternal care, I will fulfill my pledge of making you happy. I, who am the Celestial Empress, will take care of your every need, if only you will consent to live united to Me."

"I come from Heaven and invite you to enter into the Kingdom of your Mother, that is, into the Kingdom of the Divine Will. I am knocking at the door of your heart because I want you to open it to Me.

Do you realize that it is with my own hands that I'm bringing you this book as a Gift? I am offering it to you with a mother's care so that you, and your turn upon reading it, will learn to live the way of Heaven and no longer that of earth.

This Book is of gold, my child. It will become your spiritual fortune and your happiness even here while you are on earth.

In it you will find the fountain of all goods. If you are weak, you will acquire strength; If you are tempted you will conquer the temptations that come to you; If you have fallen into sin, you will fill a powerful and compassionate hand to lift you up.

If you are afflicted, you will find comfort; And if you are cold, you will be given the sure means to warm yourself; if you become hungry, you will taste the exquisite food of the Divine Will, and with it nothing will ever be lacking to you.

You will never be alone because your Mother will be your sweet companion; and with every maternal care, I will fulfill my pledge of making you happy. I, who am the Celestial Empress, will take care of your every need, if only you will consent to live united to Me."

What Does The Word 'Fiat' Mean?

FIAT is a big word in the Divine Will. Fiat is the Latin word for

'Let It Be Done'

What Does Fiat Mean?

Fiat means, Let It Be Done. It Means Yes! Let It Be Done!

Mary gave Her Fiat! And God Wants Our Fiat.

In Latin: 'Fiat Mihi, Voluntas Tuus.' Let It Be Done To Me, According To Your Will.

What is The Divine Will -versus- Divine Volition? They Can Basically Be Understood As The Same Thing. 'Will' Is The Noun- 'Volition' Is The Action Verb. So, 'Volition' Is 'The Divine Will' In Action.

When we hear the word FIAT - First of all, There Are Three Major Fiats or Works that God Gave.

What Are The Three Fiats?

The Three Major Works Of God:

The Fiat of Creation,

The Fiat of Redemption,

and The Fiat of The Divine Will – Which Is The Sanctification.

In Creation God Spoke and Said: 'FIAT Lux'

He Said, "Fiat Lux" Let There Be Light and all of Creation was Immediately Created and Spread out in the Universe.

God is Awaiting Our Fiat- In Union With Jesus' Fiat In The Garden Of Olives- Gethsemane - Which Repairs The Disobedience Of Adam And Eve.

Jesus' Fiat In The Garden Of Olives- The Garden Of Gethsemane
"Not My Will, But Thine Be Done."
Luke 22:42

Then There Is Our Lady's Fiat–
 which is referring to Her Answer To The Angel Gabriel At The Annunciation:
 "Fiat Mihi Voluntas Tua" "Let It Be Done To Me According To Your Will."

And There is Luisa Piccarreta's Fiat – In Union With Mary's And Jesus' Fiats.

And Our Fiat – That God Now Wants: Our "Let It Be Done To Me According To Your Will."

In The End It Is All Faith. It Takes Our Human Will To Learn About, Receive, And Live In the Divine Will. There Are No Outward Signs.

Defining Terms

What Is 'Divine Will' versus 'Divine Volition'?

You will read about the 'Divine Will' And the 'Divine Volition' in Luisa's Writings–
'Divine Will' and 'Divine Volition' For All Practical Purposes Mean The Same Thing: The Divine Will.

Divine Will Is the Verb– And Divine Volition Is The Action Verb.
The action verb for The Divine "Will" is The Divine "Volition".

Book Of Heaven – March 18, 1903, footnote [1] Understanding of "Divine Will and Divine Volition"; The word "Will" translates from the Italian "Volonta".

We know from the writings of Luisa that the Will of God is the boundless "container" which contains all the Acts of God, and that the Will of God and the Acts of God possess the same qualities as the Nature of God- they are Infinite, Omnipotent, Eternal, as God is.

The word "Volition" translates from the Italian "Volere". This word indicates the "will in act".

This distinction could be relevant in the case of a human will and of human acts, which are finite and limited (as they possess the same qualities as the human nature), therefore they have a beginning and an end; so we could distinguish between whether they are in act, or not.

But when we speak about will of God and volition of God, the distinction does not exist. In fact the Will of God is, yes, the "boundless container" of all the Acts of God, but we know that the Acts of God are always in act, always present, and therefore there is no distinction between whether these Acts are in act, or not- the acts of God are simply always and eternally in act.

Therefore though there may be a semantic difference between the words "will" and "volition", when referring to God any actual distinction disappears, because in God, "Will" and "Will in act" (Volition) are exactly the same.

So, when we find the two words in the Writings of Luisa, we can interpret them in the same way.

Just as in Italian, "Divina Volonta" and "Divino Volere" are used interchangeably.

What Does The Word 'Fiat' Mean?

FIAT is a big word in the Divine Will. Fiat is the Latin word for 'Let It Be Done.'

What Does Fiat Mean?
Fiat means, Let It Be. It Means Yes! Let It Be Done!

Mary gave Her Fiat!

In Latin: Fiat Mihi, Voluntas Tuus. Let It Be Done To Me, According To Your Will What is The Divine Will -versus- Divine Volition?

They Can Basically Be Understood As The Same Thing. 'Will' Is The Noun- 'Volition' Is The Action Verb. So, 'Volition' Is 'The Divine Will' In Action.

When we hear the word FIAT – First of all, There Are Three Major Fiats or Works that God Gave What Are The Three Fiats?

The Three Major Works Of God.

The Fiat of Creation The Fiat of Redemption The Fiat of The Divine Will – Which Is The Sanctification.

In Creation God Spoke and Said: 'FIAT Lux' "FIAT" Let It Be Done

He Said, "Fiat Lux" Let There Be Light and all of Creation was Immediately Created and Spread out in the Universe.

God is Awaiting Our Fiat- In Union With Jesus'

Fiat In The Garden Of Olives Which Repairs The Disobedience Of Adam And Eve.

Jesus' Fiat In The Garden Of Olives- The Garden Of Gethsemane
"Not My Will, But Thine Be Done."
Luke 22:42

Then There Is Our Lady's Fiat-
which is referring to Her Answer To The Angel Gabriel At The Annunciation

"Fiat Mihi Voluntas Tua"

"Let It Be Done To Me According To Your Will."

And There is Luisa Piccarreta's Fiat - In Union With Mary's And Jesus' Fiat.

And It Is Our Fiat That God Now Wants: Our 'Let It Be Done To Me According To Your Will'.

In The End It Is All Faith. It Takes Our Human Will To Learn About, Receive, And Live In the Divine Will.   There Are No Outward Signs.

What Does Fusing Yourself In The Divine Will Mean?

Fusing Yourself In The Divine Will Means Calling The Divine Will To Be Connected To Your Human Will And Taking Over Operational Control Of Your Human Will And Your Life.
This is What Living In The Divine Will is.

The Lost Gift

The Divine Will Is The Gift That Adam And Eve Lost and That Jesus Is Now Giving Back To Those Who Will Receive It On God's Terms.

All Of The Spiritual Life Is About The Human Will Versus the Divine Will. When We Sign Ourselves Back To The Divine Will, And God Confirms It, Our Struggle Is All Over.

Please See My Chapter: Our Lady Explains the Human Will.

The Blessed Virgin Mary's Own Words:

<u>"The creature, with its human will, is all vacillating, weak, inconstant, disordered.</u>

<u>And this is so because God, in creating it, created it united as in nature with His Divine Will in such a way that it should be the strength, the prime movement, the support, the food, the life of the human will.</u>

Thus, by not giving life to the Divine Will in ours, the goods received from God in the Creation are rejected and also the rights received in nature in the act in which we were created.

Oh, how I understood well the grave offense which is made to God and the evils which pour down upon the creature! I had such horror and fear of doing my will that justly I feared, because Adam also was created innocent by God: yet "by doing his will", into how many evils did not he and all generations plunge?"

Please Note: You may see the phrase: yet "by doing his will", - this is simply referring to someone living in the human will in a fallen state that is, all of humanity has lived in the human will - disconnected from the Fullness Of The Divine Will.

This is the original sin that changed the actual state of our soul to living disconnected from The Fullness Of The Divine Will.

There are different levels of the Divine Will:

There Is The Basic Level In Which God Keeps Everything In Existence, And then There is The Fullness Of The Divine Will. When We Are Talking About The Divine Will in Relation to Luisa

Piccarreta's Writings – We Are Referring To The "Fullness" Of The Divine Will.

The Divine Will That Luisa Piccarreta Refers To Is the Fullness Of The Divine Will Which Is The Substance and Essence Of God. This is The Source and Operative Life Of the Trinity That All Three Persons Of The Trinity Have In Common.

This Is What We Are Signing Ourselves Over To Living In Us: The Fullness Of God.

God's Presence

In The Same Sense, as With The Will Of God, There Are Different Levels Of God's Presence In Us.

There Is The Basic Level Of God Keeping Us All In Existence, And Then There Are Different Levels Of His Presence In Inanimate Objects, In Vegetation, In Animals, and In Humans.

These Are Different Levels of The Presence Of God– All The Way Up To Jesus' Presence In the Eucharist And In Those Living In The Fullness Of The Divine Will As Living Hosts– Which is The Same Real Life Presence Of Jesus; the Body Blood, Soul, and Divinity Of Our Lord Jesus Christ – Living In The "Accidents" Of The Eucharist – but living In the Acts Of Humans In The Divine Will.

The Divine Will is Jesus' Real Presence In Us

The Father Is The Divine Will.

Please See The Next Segment– How To Pray In The Divine Will. In It You Will See That **The** Father **Is The Divine Will.**

"And I put the poor creatures into safety in this Divine Will, and the Divine Father was satisfied with them. **Nor could He reject Me, being that He**

Himself is the Holy Will."

<u>**All Three Persons Of The Trinity Share In The Same Divine Will, God's Divine Will.**</u>

 I say God's Divine Will - even Though 'Divine' Means: 'Of God' - Because there Are Different Levels Of Gods Will- There is The basic Level Of The Divine Will - In which All Of the Universe Is In The Will of God- God Keeps us in Existence And Gives Us Life.
 And Then There Is The Divine Will Gift-   Which Is The Fullness Of The Divine Will- Which Is the Source And Operative Life Of the Trinity.

This is The Gift That Adam and Eve Had Before Their Fall, And What God Has Returned To Luisa Piccarreta For Her and For All Humanity.

We Just Have To Learn About It, Sign Ourselves Over To It And Live In It.

How To Pray In The Divine Will

Book Of Heaven –

Volume 11, May 3, 1916

Jesus To Luisa: While I was praying, my amiable Jesus came near; and I heard that He was also praying; and I began to listen to Him.

And Jesus said to me, "My daughter, pray; but pray as I pray. That is, pour yourself completely in my Will; and in This you will find God and all creatures.

And, making yours all the things of creatures, you will give them to God as if they were one single creature, because the Divine Will is the Master of everyone.

And, at the feet of the Divinity you will deposit the good acts to give the Divinity honor, and the bad to make reparation for them with the Sanctity, Power

<u>*and Immensity of the Divine Will from which nothing escapes.*</u>

This was the life of my humanity upon the earth. For as holy as It was, it needed this Divine Will to give complete satisfaction to the Father and to redeem the human generations; because only in this Divine Will did I find all the past, present and future generations and all their acts, thoughts, words and so forth, as in one act.

And in this Holy Will, without anything escaping Me, I took all the thoughts in my mind and brought Myself before the Supreme Majesty and repaired them for each one in particular.

And in this same Will I descended into each of the creatures minds, giving them the good that I had impenetrated for their intelligences.

In My glances I took all the creatures' eyes, in My voice their words, in My movements theirs, in My hands their works, in My heart their affections and desires, in My feet steps; and, making them like Mine, my Humanity satisfied the Father.

And I put the poor creatures into safety in this Divine Will, and the Divine Father was satisfied with them. *Nor could He reject Me, being that He Himself is the Holy Will.*

Would he perhaps reject Himself? Certainly not! All the more because in these acts, He found perfect sanctity, unattainable and enrapturing beauty, supreme love, immense and eternal acts, invincible power.
This was all the Life of my Humanity upon the earth from the first instant of my conception unto the last breath, to continue it in Heaven and in the Most Holy Sacrament.

Now, why cannot you also do it? FOR HE WHO LOVES ME, ALL IS POSSIBLE UNITED TO ME!

In my Will, pray and bring before the Divine Majesty in your thoughts the thoughts of everyone; In your eyes the glances of everyone; in your words, movements, affections, and desires those of your brothers to make reparation for them; to impenetrate light, graces and love for them. In my Will, you will find yourself in Me and in everyone. You do my Life.

You will pray with Me; And the Divine Father will be content with it; and all Heaven will say: Who calls us upon the earth? Who is it that wants to embrace this Holy Will in herself, inclosing all of us together? And how much good you can obtain for the earth by making Heaven descend upon the earth."

[You must enter into The Divine Will – to understand The Divine Will.]

[You must sign yourself over to God In His Gift Of The Divine Will – It Takes "A Firm Commitment."

It Is A Continuous Agreement With God. This is critical, As well as praying and acting in The Divine Will]

Luisa Is Fully Vetted

Luisa Has Been Fully Vetted By The Catholic Church.

You Tube: Tuesday August 13, 2024

BREAKING: Luisa Piccarreta Given Nihil Obstat by Vatican's DDF - Cause For Canonization Ongoing!
@ Daniel O'Connor   Communication Of The Postulator Msgr. Paolo Rizzi about the Cause Of Beatification

Daniel O'Connor: I just want to share a brief update with some very good news.

The Servant of God Luisa Piccarreta just had Her Cause For Beatification and Canonization receive a Vatican Nihil Obstat From The- DDF –

That Is The Vatican's Dicastery Of The Doctrine Of The Faith, and remember, A DDF Nihil Obstat is today the highest level of approval that the Church gives to any private revelation...

...Luisa has been a Church approved Mystic for over 100 years. I mean this was the case over 100 years ago when St. Annibale Di Francia gave 19 Nihil Obstats to her revelations and the Archbishop followed up in 19 Imprimaturs Of His Own and we can continue moving on here, it became even more legitimate to refer to her as a Church approved Mystic when in the 1990s the Church declared her Servant of God. Her Cause for Canonization Beautification opened up. There you can see some images from it when later still in 2011 a religious order explicitly dedicated to Luisa's revelations was approved by The Church. (The Benedictines Of The Divine Will)...

Also See Luisa Piccarreta Official Website Luisapiccarretaofficial.org The Nihil Obstat for the resumption of the Cause Of Beatification of The Servant Of God Luisa Piccarreta has been issued. This was announced by the Postulator Of The Cause, Msgr. Paola Rizzi, in a note dated August 10, 2024, the text of which is published here. (on the website) The cause of Beatification of The Servant of God Luisa Piccarreta has never been closed, but has always been pending at the Dicastery For The Causes Of Saints...

The Catholic Saints Are The Modern Day Prophets And All Lead Up To Luisa Piccarreta.

Saint Annibale De Francia Confirmed Luisa As A Very Holy Person In Her Time. Gave The "Nihil Obstat" – The "All Clear From Any Doctrinal Or Moral Errors." on The First 19 Volumes Of Her Writings -All That Were Available At The Time Of

His Death; And Published Luisa's Book The Hours Of The Passion of Our Lord –

And When He Read From This Book To Pope Pius X, The Pope Said, "Let Us Get On Our Knees When Reading This Book," These Are The Words Of Jesus Himself. Pope Benedict XVI And Pope John Paul II Actively Promoted Her Writings And The Cause For Her Beatification.

The Vatican Has Confirmed The "Nihil Obstat" By Two Vatican Appointed Theologians For Cause of The Servant Of God Luisa Piccarreta Who Scoured Through All Of Her Writings In The 2020's And Gave Them The 'All Clear From Any Doctrinal or Moral Errors.'

This Is What God Is Calling Us To In This Hour On Earth, To Dive In And Listen To What The Greatest Of Our Modern Day Prophets Is Telling Us.

The Process Of The Application Of Luisa Piccarreta 1994: The Vatican gave "Non Obstare" to Mons. Carmelo Casati, Archbishop of Trani-Barletta Bisceglia to start the cause of beatification and Luisa Piccarreta automatically became a Servant of God.

November 20, 1994: the cause of beatification was opened officially on the Feast Of Christ The King.

January 1996: Then Cardinal Ratzinger now Pope Benedict XV I released 34 Volumes Of The Book Of Heaven to Archbishop Cassati as part of the protocol for process of Luisa's Cause of Beatification.

March 1997: on the occasion of the 50th anniversary of Luisa's death, it was announced publicly that the Tribunal Responsible For of Luisa's Cause had determined unanimously that her life was one of heroic virtue and that her mystical experiences were authentic.

October 28, 2005: The cause of the edification was officially concluded at the diocesan phase.

November 7, 2005: All the official documents were transferred to the Vatican.

March 7, 2006: Congregation for the Causes of Saints opened the box (started the cause) officially.

2008: Congregation for the Causes of Saints appointed two independent, highly qualified theologians- Fr. Antonio Resta, President of the Pontifical Theological Seminary in Italy; Fr, Cosimo Reh, dogmatic theologian- to review Luke of Luisa's writings.

End of 2009: One of two theologians gave his positive judgment.

July 19, 2010: The other theologian gave his positive judgment.

Positive Judgment means that there are no teachings in of Luisa's writings contrary to Catholic Faith and Morals.

It also means that the Church recognizes the legitimacy and authenticity of her writings.

What is the Church's stance on Luisa Piccarreta?

Since she has not yet been declared Venerable, there is nothing that yet amounts to formal Vatican "approval" of Luisa's writings.

Vatican's the current, official position on of Luisa's sanctity and her writings is neutral. The Catholic Church does not yet officially give them her full "approval" but neither does she "condemn" them.

The Archbishop promoting Luisa's cause is doing so in strict accord with Canon law and in complete harmony with Rome. This includes a careful and comprehensive review of Luisa's writings by competent, independent experts in theology.

In summary, the record is entirely clear concerning the writings of Luisa. Anyone can read them with a clear conscience and be completely at peace."

My Entire Hope In Writing This Book Is To Give You A Basic Understanding Of The Divine Will, But To Get You To Read The Writings Of Luisa.

God Is Not A Trickster. There Is God's Power In Every Word Of The Book Of Heaven. And If You Read The Bible, Then You Will Recognize That Same Jesus Speaking In Luisa'a Writings.

POPE Pius X CONFIRM THIS ABOUT LUISA. If A Person Has Any Doubts About Whether Or Not This Is Really Jesus Speaking And Giving This Gift, Then Dig In And Find Out!

Read The Bible, And The Lives Of the Catholic Saints, And The Apparitions Of The Blessed Virgin Mary– They All Lead Us To Luisa And Prepare Us to Receive The Greatest Gift That God Can Ever Give Creatures – The Gift Of the Divine Will.

Jesus makes it clear in the writings, that We Humbly Submit To The Authority Of The Catholic Church On Luisa's Cause For Sainthood – And It Is No Accident That These Writings Are Now Being Released Right Now On The Internet For Us To Gather Them In When We Need Them Most!

The Summit Of Human History

We Are At the Summit Of Human History – All Cycles Come Together In Our Time, And Then Again At The End Of The Millennium Of Peace.

This coincides with all the writings of the Patriarchs Of The Old Testament And Catholic Saints Of The New Testament Times, for the past 2,000 years – which have all led up to this Gift of the Divine Will and all Coincide with the Approved Apparitions of the Blessed Virgin that have been happening and that promise us the Era of Peace.

The Blessed Virgin At Fatima said that, in the end, Her Immaculate Heart Will Triumph and that an Era Of Peace would be Granted To The World; (see blue army. com)

Satan is being vanquished and chained for a thousand years in The Gift Of The Divine Will – As we are coming through The Purification And Into The Millennium of Peace.

We Have Come To Understand that This Gift of the Divine Will And The Era Of Peace is the Triumph of Her Immaculate Heart.

God's Plan Is Huge!

And Covers All Of Human History.

Did You Not Think That Jesus Would Appear And Reclaim The Earth And Humanity From Satan's Reign? We Live In That Time.

This Is The Whole Focus Of Human History And The Bible, But Few Understand It.

All Of Humanity Is The Prodigal Son.

All Of Human History Is God Preparing Humans To Return Home – With The Return Of The Gift Of The Divine Will That Adam And Eve Lost.

Every 2,000 Years Is A Purification. God Has To Cleanse The Earth And Start Over.

In The First 2,000 Years Was The Physical Purification By Flood, and Then the Redemption, And A Spiritual Purification; And Now In Our Time, This Is The Sanctification- Both a Spiritual and A Physical Purification

At Noah's Time Was The Chastisement Of Water. Noah's Ark Had To Be Sealed Against Water. In Our Day, Sin And Death Are Raining Down Upon The Earth.

The Problem Today Is Sin- Our Refuge - Our Ark Today Has To Be Sealed Against Sin And Death. It's Mary The Sinless Ark. Our Lady Is the Gift Of The Divine Will For Us.

Sin Has Become A Way Of Life. We All Live A Society Against The Divine Order. This is Not Peace But Chaos.

It's Spiritual Warfare.

We Are Living With A Defective Nature With Our Human Will Running Our Souls – On Its Own!

Human Beings Were Never Intended To Have Our Human Wills In Charge Of Our Souls - ON ITS OWN!

Satan has Successfully Infiltrated The Human Society.

We Are Living In A Society: Where We Are Doing Everything That Christ Told Us Not To Do.

In Which Virtues Have Become Vices, And Vices Have Become Virtues. We Have All Been Part Of This Culture Of Death. Today's Society Has Become Similar To The Death Culture In Mexico Before The Virgin Of Guadalupe Appeared And There Was The Greatest Mass Conversion To Christianity.

Today The World Is Being Cleansed Of Sin.

God Must Cast Out All Humans Continuing To be Willingly Infected And Infested With Evil.

God Always Preserves A Remnant.

God Must Protect The Seed Of Abraham. The Seed Is Jesus, The Son Of God.

Satan is the destroyer —of the character Of God In Us. Evil Has Infiltrated Our Very Nature And In This Way Our World.

The Demon Angels And The Fallen Humans Are Joining Forces Right Now Before Our Eyes To Make A Last Stand Against The Seed Of Jesus. In Today's Society, Human Beings Are Living For Ourselves, In A Society Without God.

The Following Stanzas Are Adapted From The Movie Pope John Paul II:

They say that they are bringing us freedom, but a society without God, will never bring us freedom, not for us or for anyone.

They have created a religion; a religion that is based on man at the center.

And God? For today's society, He does not exist. Nor does the human soul.

They have created God in their own image. He is whatever they want Him to be. They say that they are for the individual, but only if he will give up his freedom, and substitute God for what they allow.

Our True Freedom Is To Sign Ourselves Over To God's Divine Will.

The Line Of David Is Being Attacked Again, In Us

God's Messengers and *Prophets and Saints Have Warned Us That If We Don't Change, That A Terrible Chastisement Is Upon Us.*

We have God's Spirit striving with humanity today, and we are grieving God's Spirit by all the evil that we're doing.

Only A Remnant Will Survive.

God Has Provided The Spiritual Ark For Us As Refuge.

It Is The Sinless Blessed Virgin Mary, The Golden Ark – Under Her Greatest Title: "Our Lady, Queen And Mother Of The Divine Will."

We Are The Most Blessed People To Have Ever Been Born, Because We Are Living Right Now On Earth When This Gift Is Known And Available.

This Gift Is Our Refuge From The Impending Cataclysmic Events Which Have Begun

– Jesus Told Luisa:

"...Most Of This Generation Will Be Destroyed."

"The Survivors Will Be Few..."

"...After This I Will Be Even More Generous With Creatures."

Jesus Told Luisa That The Greatest Sign That The Era Of Peace Is Coming To The Earth Is That I Have Appeared To This Soul, Luisa Piccarreta, Like I Appeared To My Mother For The Redemption.

The Most Noble Act

This Is Purgatory Ahead Of Time, As We Enter Into Living In The Divine Will.

Jesus Told Luisa That He Could Not Allow The Fire Of Purgatory To Touch Someone Who Lived In The Divine Will.

BOOK OF HEAVEN

Volume 11 – March 14, 1914

... "So, as she lives and dies in my Volition, there is no good which she does not carry with herself, because there is no good which my Will does not contain; My will is the life of all the good that creatures can do. **Therefore is the soul who dies in my Will, she carries with her the Masses that are celebrated, and the prayers and the good works that are done, because they are all fruits of my Will.**

And this is still very little compared to the operating of my Will Itself which the soul carries within her as her own.

One instant of the operating of my Will is enough to surpass all the works of all creatures, past, present and future.

So as the soul dies in my Will there is no beauty that matches her, no nor heights, riches, sanctity, wisdom or love; nothing – nothing can equal her.

As the soul who dies in my Will enters into the Heavenly Fatherland, not only will the Heaven's gates open, but the entire Heaven will bow to welcome her into the celestial dwelling, to honor the workings of my Will.

"What should I tell you, then, of the feast and the surprise of all the Blessed in seeing this soul completely marked by the workings of the Divine Will;

In seeing, in this soul who has done everything in my Will, that everything she has done during her life- each saying, each thought, word, work, action of hers – are many suns that adorn her, each one different from the other in light and in beauty; *and in seeing in this soul many divine rivulets that will inundate all the Blessed and flow also upon earth for the good of pilgrim souls, since Heaven cannot contain them.*"

...." Ah, my daughter, my will is the portent of portents. It is the secret to finding light, sanctity and riches – it is the secret to all goods; but it is not known, and therefore not appreciated nor loved. You at least, appreciate it, love it, and make it known to those whom you see disposed."

...." Another day he told me: "My daughter, one who does my Will can by no means go to Purgatory, because my Will purges the soul of everything.

After keeping her so jealously during her life, and the custody of my volition, how could I allow the fires of purgatory to touch her? At the most she may lack some clothing, but my will, before revealing the divinity to her, will clothe her in all that she may lack. And then I reveal myself."

BOOK OF HEAVEN –

Volume 12 – July 25, 1917

The Divine Will Instantly Purifies and Enriches the Soul in the Act of Entering Into the Divine Volition

Jesus To Luisa: "**You must know that the most noble, most sublime, most grand, most heroic act is to do my Will and operate in my Volition. Therefore, no other act can equal this act.**

I make a display of all My Love and Generosity. Scarcely does the soul decide to do it, then I give her the honor of holding her in My Volition, in that act in which the two volitions encounter each other to fuse themselves one in the other to form One alone.

If she is stained, I purify her; if the thorns of human nature envelop her, I break them; and if some nail transfixes her, that is sin, I pulverize it because nothing of evil can enter into My Will. Indeed, all My Attributes invest her and change weakness into strength, ignorance into knowledge, misery into riches and so with all the rest.

And in the other acts there remains always something of one's self, but these acts are completely despoiled of one's self; **and I fill her all with Me."**

(For The Full Quote - See The Section Titled: The Greatest Thing)

The Three Fiats

The Three Fiats Are The Three Major Works Of God: Creation, Redemption, and The Sanctification.

We Are Living In The Time Of The Third Fiat Which Is The Sanctification.

The Gift of the Divine Will is not just a Gift for man, it is a Gift for all of Creation.

The Sanctification Is A New Heaven and a New Earth.

Romans 8:19 NRSV

"For the Creation waits in eager longing for the revealing of The Sons of God."

Fall In Love With God Anew!

Let The Divine Will Flow In And Through You.

Jeremiah 30:17 KJV

"For I will restore health unto thee, and I will heal thee of thy wounds, saith the LORD; because they called thee an Outcast, saying, This is Zion, whom no man seventh after. Let us rejoice and be glad and give him glory. For the wedding day of the lamb has come, his bride has made herself ready."

(Rev. 19: 7)

"I also saw the holy city, a new Jerusalem, coming down out of heaven from God, prepared as a bride adorned for her husband."

(Rev. 21: 2)

"He took me in spirit to a great, high mountain and so the holy city Jerusalem coming down out of heaven from God."

(Rev. 21:10)

"But the Jerusalem above is freeborn, and she is our mother."

(Galatians 4: 26)

The New Jerusalem. The City Of God. "The "New Jerusalem' is a symbol of the Church, the bride of Christ. As such it exists both in Heaven and on Earth through the communion of Saints. At the Last Judgement it will exist in the transformed world through the Resurrection."

www.catholic.com – Fr. Charles Grondin

Where Is the New Jerusalem? - Fr. Charles Grondin The Church Is The New Jerusalem. The New Jerusalem Is Descending from Heaven To The Earth In The Divine Will To Usher In The Millennium Of Peace.

A Restoration Of Mankind

The Divine Will Is Not Just Some Devotion. It Is The Fulfillment And Capstone Of The New Covenant.

It Is The Actual Source And Power And Life Of The Holy Trinity In Heaven Coming Into Us.

It Is The Power That Generates And Runs The Trinity And We Are Plugged Back Into It – In – And Through The Power Of The Divine Will, Which Is God Himself Is "Our Rising" To A New Divine Life.

What The Enemy Meant For Evil– "The Fall" Of Adam And Eve – Is Being Used For Good– "Our Rising" To A New Life –Even Greater Than Before The Fall.

Humanity Is Returning Home To Live A Renewed Life And A New Era Of Peace. God Is Inviting Us Back Home And Makes Us Whole.

Jesus Appeared To Luisa Piccarreta And Explained The Problem With The Human Condition - And Gave Her the Cure - For Her And For All Of Humanity.

The Gift Of Living In The Divine Will Is The Only Way To Heal Our Fallen Human Nature And Make It Whole Again! This Divine Will Is God's Own Will.

God Is Healing Our Human Nature If We Want—Jesus Asked, Do You Want To Be Healed?

"Wilt Thou Be Made Whole?" John 5:6

We Learn In The Book Of Heaven

That This Is Our Birthright And Our Heritage To Live In The Divine Will.

This Is Normal Human Living relying on God, the way God intended from the beginning—before the fall.

By His Own Promises, God Cannot Deny Us To Live In The Divine Will. And God Cannot Deny Someone Their Requests Who Is Living In The Divine Will- For He Cannot Turn Down His Own Will.

Now We Understand Why God Cannot Turn Down Our Lady's Requests.
The Blessed Virgin Mary Lived Her Entire Life On Earth And Now In Heaven In The Divine Will.

God Heals Our Human Nature In The Gift Of Living In The Divine Will.

This Divine Will Is The Specific And Practical Way That We Enter Into God.

We Enter Into God: Human Will To Divine Will.

This Is Our Test

It Does Not Matter What You Have Done Up Until Now.

Our Test Is To Learn About, Receive, And Live In The Gift Of The Divine Will– All The Rest Of Our Lives On Earth And Then In Heaven.

Adam And Eve Had A Test.

Their Test Was To Stay Living In The Gift Of The Divine Will. They Disobeyed And Pulled Their Human Will Out Of The Fullness Of The Divine Will.

And This Is How All Humans Have Lived Ever Since, With Our Human Will Running Our Lives – Outside Of The Fullness Of The Divine Will.

This is What A Fallen Nature Is.

(All Humans Have Lived As Fallen Human Beings, Except Jesus And Mary Who Lived Their Entire Lives In The Divine Will, And Luisa Piccarreta Who Was Given The Gift Of The Divine Will, And All Those Who Have Learned And Lived The Divine Will From Her.)

God Is Not Done With Humanity.
All Of Human History Has Been To Prepare Us To Receive This Gift Back Again.

God's Plan All Along Has Been To Give Us Back The Gift That Adam and Eve Lost.

God's Plan Is To Raise Us Up From Living In A Defective Fallen Nature, To Living "A New And Divine Life."

The Great Event

This Gift Is Not Just For Humans, But For The Entire Earth.

This Is Why The Messiah Came To Give Us the New Covenant, And The Divine Will Is The Completion Of The New Covenant.

We Are Living In The Time Of The Middle Coming Of Jesus–

 Which Will Result In 'The Great Event' Of The Era Of Peace.

This Living In The Gift Of The Divine Will Is The Only Way To Solve Our Problems And Heal Our Human Nature, and Earth.

This Gift Of Living In The Divine Will Is The Divine Life That Adam And Eve Lost – And Has Been Given Back To Humanity. God Is Ushering In The Era Of

Peace Upon The Earth Right Now– In Those Who Are Taking Up Living In the Divine Will.

God Has Safeguarded This Gift

God Is Not Going To Give Us This Gift, Which Is His Divine Possession, If There Is Any Chance, We Will Betray Him, Like The Fallen Angels Did, And Adam And Eve Did.

We Take It On Loan At First While We Are Transformed In Grace.

Once We Are Living In The Divine Will, And God Decides That We Are Trustworthy, Then He Will Confirm Us In This Gift On Earth And For Eternity In Heaven.

This Gift Is The Fulfillment Of The New Covenant:

For I will restore health to you, and your wounds I will heal, says the Lord. And you shall be my people, and I will be your God.

(Jeremiah 30:17, 22)

The Kingdom Of Heaven Is A Divine Indwelling!

We Sign Ourselves Over – Directly To God To Live In Us In This Gift Of The Divine Will.

This Is The Promised Sanctification Of Humanity.

We Sign Ourselves Over To This Divine Gift And We Enter In, And God takes Over Complete Control Of Us, It Happens Instantaneously–But It's Still A Process.

This is the fastest, quickest, and most efficient way to become Holy, but it's still a process.

We Must Begin To Interiorly Call Jesus Into Doing All Our Acts, And To Accept Everything He Sends Us– But This Does Not Mean We Become Doormats For Others.

The Knowledge Of The Divine Will Is Preeminent.

At First, God Strips Us Of All Attachments To The Human Will- This Is Our Purgatory ahead Of Time.

If We Are Sincere, and Understand How Astounding This Gift Is, We Will Keep Calling Jesus To Do All Our Actions – Because We Know That He Is Our Only Consolation. We Must Be Persistent And Dogged In Signing Ourselves Over To The Divine Will- and Clinging To God. This Becomes Our Continuous Act.

Jesus, You Do It In Me.

We Come Through A Rough Period In The Beginning Depending On How Willing We Are To Let God Strip Us Of All Attachments To The Human Will- And Count It All A Blessing!

This Is The Kingdom Of God Descending From Heaven To Earth In Those Taking Up Living In The Divine Will. This Gift In Individuals Will Culminate, After The Purification, In The Era Of Peace For The Whole Earth.

The New Covenant

For God To Give Us The New Covenant- Is A Two Step Process, Which Merges Into One.

First Is The Redemption, and Now Is The Sanctification.

The Redemption Is Salvation, And The Sanctification Is Perfection.

Most Christians Claim Salvation, But Miss the Completion Of Salvation, Which Is To Be Made Holy- The Sanctification.

1 Thessalonians 5:23 – KJV

"And the very God of peace sanctify you wholly; and I pray God your whole spirit and soul and body be preserved blameless unto the coming of our Lord Jesus Christ."

Did You Ever Wonder: If Jesus Came To Restore The Kingdom, Then Why Is There Still Sin And Death?

Jesus Told Luisa That He Had To Take Us From The Lesser To The Greater Knowledge Of God And Man. Jesus Explained To Luisa That Humans Were Not Prepared To Receive The Sanctification- Which Is The Living In The Divine Will - When He Was On Earth 2,000 Years Ago.

Jesus Gave Us The Redemption: The Church, the Sacraments, and The Saints Of The Catholic Church And Has Appeared And Given Messages Over the Past 2,000 years All To Prepare Us For This Gift.

Now, In Our Day, Humanity Is Disposed To Receive The Gift Of The Divine Will, Which Is Our Sanctification.

We Have The Knowledge Of Jesus' Life, Death, and Resurrection. We Have The Knowledge Of The Bible And Know That We Can Trust Completely In Jesus Who Died On The Cross To Save Us And Sanctify Us.

Every One Of Us Is Prepared. We Just Have To Learn About It, Sign Ourselves Over To It, And Live In It.

The Middle Coming

Mark Mallet.com/blog/the-middle-coming

"The Sabbath Rest "

"Jesus often taught that the "Kingdom of Heaven is at hand."

"Moreover he taught us to pray, "Thy Kingdom Come, Thy Will be done on Earth as it is in Heaven."

"Thus St. Bernard sheds more light on this hidden coming.

In case someone should think that what we say about this middle coming is sheer invention, listen to what our Lord Himself says: if anyone loves me he will keep my word, and my Father will love him, and we will come to him – Saint Bernard, Liturgy of the Hours, Vol 1, p. 169

The "Kingdom of God" then, is intrinsically tied to the "Will of God." as Pope Benedict said:

...we recognize that "Heaven" is where the Will of God is Done, and that "earth" becomes "Heaven" - ie, the place of the presence of love, of goodness, of truth and of divine beauty - if only on earth the will of God is done-

POPE BENEDICT XVI, General Audience, February 1st, 2012, Vatican City

[HOW IS THE WILL OF GOD DONE ON EARTH AS IN HEAVEN?

IN THOSE LIVING IN THE GIFT OF THE DIVINE WILL!]

Mark Mallet.com/blog/the-middle-coming

"On the one hand, we can observe the coming of Christ throughout the Church's 2,000-year history, most especially in His Saints and in the renewals that their particular Fiats brought.

However, The Middle Coming we are referring to here is an ushering in of the "age of the Spirit", in an era in which, corporately as a Body, the Church will live in the Divine Will "on earth as it is in heaven".

It will be as close to Heaven as the Church will get without the beatific vision.

It is a union of the same nature as that of the union of heaven, except that in paradise the veil which conceals the Divinity disappears...

(Jesus to Venerable Conchita, Ronda Chervin, Walk with me Jesus; – cited in The Crown and Completion of All Sanctities, Daniel O'Connor, p.12.)

And thus, in such union, the Church Fathers foresaw that this era would also be "a rest" when the people of God having labored six days (ie. "six thousand years") will rest on the seventh day, a kind of "sabbath" for the Church.

Because this [middle] coming lies between the other two, it is like a road on which we travel from the first coming to the last.

In the first, Christ was our redemption; in the last, he will appear as our life; in this middle coming, he is our rest and consolation...

In his first coming Our Lord came in our flesh and in our weakness; in this middle coming he comes in spirit and power; in the final coming he will be seen in glory and majesty...-

(St. Bernard, Liturgy of the Hours, Vol 1,p.169)

Bernard's theology is consonant with the Early Church Fathers who foretold that this rest would come after the death of the "lawless one" ushering in ... ... the times of the kingdom, that is the rest, the hallowed seventh day...

These are to take place in the times of the Kingdom, that is, upon the seventh day... the true Sabbath of the righteous–

(St. Irenaeus of Lyons, Church Father (140–202AD); Adversus Haereses, Irenaeus of Lyons Lyons, V.33-3-4, The Fathers of the Church, CIMA Publishing Co.)

... when His Son will come and destroy the time of the lawless one and judge the godless, and change the sun and the moon and the stars –

then He shall indeed rest on the seventh day...

after giving rest to all things, I will make the beginning of the eighth day, that is, the beginning of another world.–

(Letter of Barnabas (70 to 79 AD), written by a second century Apostolic Father

The Kingdom Comes In Darkness

"Dear young people, it is up to you to be the watchman of the morning who will announce the coming of the sun who is the Risen Christ "–

(POPE JOHN PAUL II, Message of the Holy Father to the Youth of the World, XVII World Youth Day n. 3; cf Is. 21:11-12)

But this coming, as so many of the popes have said, is not the end of the world, but the accomplishment of the plans of redemption.

Thus, we are to be... watchmen who proclaim to the world a new dawn of hope, brotherhood and peace –

(POPE JOHN PAUL II, Address to the Guanelli Youth Movement, April 20th, 2002, www.vatican.va)

If Our Lady is the dawn that heralds the coming "sun of justice", then when exactly does this "new Pentecost" take place?

The answer is almost as difficult as pinpointing as when the first ray of dawn begins.

After all, Jesus said: The coming of the Kingdom of God cannot be observed, and no one will announce, look, here it is, or there it is, for behold the Kingdom of God is among you. (Luke 17: 20 – 21)

That said, certain approved prophetic revelations and the scriptures themselves combined to give an insight into approximately when the "temporal Kingdom" begins to be ushered in – and it points to this third millennium.

The Kingdom Of God

The Kingdom Of God Is Now Being Revealed To The Whole Earth! –

[It's In Those Who Are Living In The Gift Of The Divine Will]

"The Church of the Millennium must have an increased consciousness of being the Kingdom of God in its initial stage…"

(POPE JOHN PAUL II, L'Osservatore Romano, English Edition, April 25th,1988 Lazuli tour Romano, English edition, April 25th 1988)

"In Revelation 12, we read of the confrontation between the Woman and the dragon. She is laboring to give birth to a "son"– that is, laboring for the middle coming of Christ.

<u>This woman represents Mary, the Mother of the Redeemer, but she represents at the same time the Whole Church, the People of God of all times, the</u>

<u>*Church that at all times, with great pain, again gives birth to Christ.*</u>"

(POPE JOHN PAUL II, Castle Gandolfo, Italy, Aug 23, 2006, Zenit)

The Church

Jesus Is Giving Us The Knowledge That Will Save The Church.

The Church Is Identified With Mary- The Church Is Giving Birth!

This is the Second Generation Of The Children Of Light!

Mary Is The Only Human Person To Have Lived Her Entire Life In The Divine Will.

Mary Is Giving Birth To Those Who are Living In The Divine Will!

(Jesus Is human And God, and He is A Divine Person.)

Mark Mallet.com/blog/the-middle-coming

"Again I've [Mark Mallet] written in detail about this battle between the woman and the dragon over the past four centuries in my book – The Final Confrontation and in other places here.

However the dragon who attempts to devour the child, fails.

"She gave birth to a son, a male child, destined to rule all the nations with an iron rod. Her child was caught up to God in his throne."

(Rev 12: 5)

"While this is a reference to Christ's Ascension, it also refers to the spiritual ascension of the Church.

As Saint Paul taught, the Father "has raised us up with Him and seated us with Him in the Heavens in Jesus Christ OUR PROMISED GIFT."

This Is The Middle Coming Of Jesus

That Is Promised By The Bible And Catholic Saints.

This Is What The Apparitions Of The Blessed Virgin Mary Are All About. To Prepare Us To Receive Jesus Interiorly And Have Him Take Over Control Of Our Lives. The Divine Indwelling Is Jesus In Us.

God Is Giving Us New Hearts Of Flesh – New Wineskins And Pouring Out The Fullness Of The Holy Spirit Over All Flesh,

But We Need New Hearts Of Flesh– New Wineskins To Receive This New Wine!

This Is The Second Pentecost.

This Is The Second Creation.

This Is The Eucharistic Reign Of Jesus Christ On Earth As In Heaven.

The Trinity Takes Up Their Abode In Us.

The Trinity Fuses The Divine Will With Our Human Will As We Sign Over And Fuse Our Human Will To The Divine Will.

We Sign Over All Rights of Our Human Will To God, And He Takes Over Control Of Our Human Will And Life In All Things.

We Continuously Call Jesus Into Doing All Our Acts In Us With His Divine Will–

The Father's Will

All Three Divine Persons Of The Trinity Have The Same Divine Will And Wants Us Humans To Participate Living That Same Divine Life Shared By The Trinity – In Jesus, And Mary, And Luisa.

We Become Living Hosts Of The Living God.

This All Happens In And Through Those Few Generous Souls Who Choose To Receive And Sign Over Their Lives To This Divine Possession.

And To Live In The Divine Will - Calling Jesus Into Doing All Our Acts- And Giving A return Of Love To The Father With His Own Will.

Those Who Die In The Divine Will Go To Heaven, And Will Be In The Highest Places In Heaven.

There Are Only Two Ways To Live, And The One Is Coming To A Halt- The Living In A Fallen Nature.

We Are Just Before The Greatest Purification That Has Ever Happened On Earth - Greater Than The Deluge;

And God Gave Us A New And Higher Way To Live To Get Through It.

This Is Another Higher Divine Life That Is The Other Way To Live That God Has Now Made Available To All Humans Now Living On The Earth.

That Is The Living In The Fullness Of The Divine Will That Jesus Gave As Gift And Our Refuge For Right Now On Earth.

The Importance Of The Knowledge

The Following Is Quoted from the Epilogue Of The Book: I Bring You Tidings Of Great Joy (Luke 2,10) 4th Edition (A work of Fr. Pablo Martin – Civitavecchia 1992) Selection of Passages about the Divine Will taken from the writings of Luisa Piccarreta "The Little Daughter of the Divine Will"

The Last Supper Discourse

Saint Paul prayed that we would have a full knowledge of The Divine Will with every knowledge and spiritual intelligence.

And Our Lord, at The Last Supper, said: "many things I have yet to say to you, but for the moment you are not capable of bearing the weight of them.

But when *The Spirit of Truth* will come, He will guide you in the truth, whole, all entire, because

He will not speak of Himself, but will say all that He has heard and will announce to you future things." (John 16,12-13).

To that end, He prayed to the Father, saying, "I have made known your name to them, and I will make it known *so that the love with which you have loved Me may be in them and I in them.*" (John 17, 26.)

It is evident how important is the Knowledge."

God Is Claiming Victory, Even Now!

The World Is Falling Down Around Us, But Even Now God Is Claiming Victory In Those Entering Into His Refuge On Earth.

God Is Pouring Himself Out In Those Who Are Taking Up The Living In The Divine Will- And Preparing Those To Live In The Era Of Peace For The Whole World That Will Arise After The

Purification And Chastisement That Has Begun On The Earth.

The Last Supper Discourse Promises A Future Grace – A Future Revelation Of Christ.

Luisa Is Our Greatest Modern Day Prophet And Received The Longest Documented Visitation Of Jesus To A Soul – Since His Coming 2,000 Years Ago.

John 13:20 – NRSV

"Very truly, I tell you, whoever receives one whom I send receives me; and whoever receives me receives him who sent me."

John 14:10-14 – NRSV

"Do you not believe that I am in the Father and the Father is in me? The words that I say to you I do not speak on my own; but the Father who dwells in me does his works. Believe me that I am in the Father and the Father is in me; But if you do not, then believe me because of the works themselves. Very truly, I tell you, the one who believes in me will also do the works that I do and, in fact will do greater works than these, because I am going to the Father.

I will do whatever you ask in my name, so that the Father may be glorified in the Son. *If in my name you ask me for anything, I will do it.'"*

(God cannot turn down anyone in His Own Divine Will, For He Cannot Turn Down Himself)

The Promise of The Holy Spirit

John 14:15-26 – NRSV

"If you love me, you will keep my commandments. And I will ask the Father, And he will give you another Advocate, to be with you forever. This is The Spirit of Truth, whom the world cannot receive, because it neither sees Him nor knows Him. You know Him, because He abides with you, and He will be in you. Jesus answered him, those who love me will keep my word, and my Father will love them, *and We will come to them and make our home with them. I have said these things to you while I am still with you. But the Advocate, The Holy Spirit, whom the Father will send in my name, will teach you everything, and remind you of all that I have said to you.*"

John 16:12 – NRSV

"I still have many things to say to you, but you cannot bear them now. When The Spirit Of Truth comes, He will guide you into all the Truth; for He will not speak on His own, but will speak whatever He hears, and He will declare to you the things that are to come."

John 17:25-26 – NRSV

"Righteous Father, the world does not know You, but I know You; and these know that You have sent me. I made your name known to them, *and I will make it known, so that the love with which you have loved me may be in them, and I in them.*"

(We Love With Jesus' Own Love)

Jesus, At The Last Supper Explains This To Us. 'I go and prepare a place for you.' 'The Holy Spirit Will Come And Explain This To You.'

This Is The Second Pentecost!

The Divine Will Gift In Us- Makes It All Possible.

All of human history, All the Structure of History- Is God shepherding us – From Doing God's Will To Living In God's Will.

God Can Only Give Himself Completely!

God Is Revealing Himself More And More Completely And Giving Himself As Gift To Us

All Of Human History Is God's Revelation To Man And Is Prelude To Jesus Appearing To Luisa Piccarreta And Returning The Gift Of The Divine Will To Her – For Her – And For All Of Humanity.

You Must Know That When Jesus Reveals Himself, He Gives Himself As Gift.

In The Last Supper Discourse,

Jesus said you do not know me yet, but when I come again, I will reveal more of myself; I will pour out The Holy Spirit and Give Myself To You.

Jesus Has Fulfilled His Promises In Dictating The Book Of Heaven To Luisa Piccarreta And Giving Her The Gift Of The Powerful Healing Of The Divine Will For Her And For All Humanity.

Luisa Gave Her Fiat- Her 'Let It Be Done To Me' - And God Is Awaiting Our Fiat!

This Is All God's Great Mercy! God Is Recreating Us In The Divine Will And Giving Us New Hearts And Pouring Out The Fullness Of The Holy Spirit. God Is Speaking To Us Today.

Ezekiel 36: 22-28 KJV

Therefore say unto the House of Israel, Thus sayeth the LORD GOD; I do not this for your sakes, O house of Israel, but for mine holy name's sake, which ye have profaned among the heathen, whither ye went.

And I will sanctify my great name, which was profaned among the heathen, which ye have profaned in the midst of them; and the heathen shall know that I am the LORD, sayeth the LORD GOD, when I shall be sanctified in you before their eyes.

[The Divine Will Is the Sanctification Of Humanity]

For I will take you from among the heathen, and gather you out of all countries, and I will bring you into your own land.

Then will I sprinkle clean water upon you, and ye shall be clean: from all your filthiness, and from all your idols, will I cleanse you.

A new heart also will I give you, and a new spirit will I put within you: and I will take away the stony heart out of your flesh, and I will give you an heart of flesh.

And I will put my spirit within you, and cause you to walk in my statutes, and ye shall keep my judgments, and do them. And ye shall dwell in the land that I gave to your fathers; and ye shall be my people, and I shall be your God. [The Era Of Peace.]

The Chosen People

All Of The Patriarchs Of Old And The Saints Over The Past 2,000 years All Wanted To Live In Our Time Right Now On Earth.

You And I Are The Most Blessed Humans To Have Ever Been Alive On The Earth Because This Biblically Promised Gift Has Been Given And We Can All Receive It.

All Of Human History Has Been Prelude To- And Has Prepared Us To Receive This Gift Of The Divine Will-

God Is Offering All Humans Now Alive This Gift Of A New And Higher Divine Existence And He Will Not Save Us Without Our Cooperation - And Right Now We Need Salvation And The Sanctification Which Is The Gift Of Living In The Divine Will.

Creation And The Redemption Are Not Finished Until The Sanctification Is Completed.

Jesus Told Luisa That The Divine Will It Is Late In Being Known.

God Is Gathering His Remnant From The Four Corners Of The Earth To Receive This Gift And Bring Us Home.

At This Time In History, We All Know How Jesus Sacrificed Himself For Us–

So We Can Trust In Jesus Completely.

We All have Been Living In A Fallen Nature – When The Gift Of The Divine Will has Been Available To Humanity–

Many Never Researched What Jesus has Been Saying To The Catholic Saints – His Modern Day Prophets– Or We Would Have Been Introduced To Luisa Piccarreta And The Urgency For Humans To Live In The Gift Of the Divine Will – Before Now.

Luisa Died In 1947. The Beatification Cause Of The Servant Of God Luisa Piccarreta Was Opened In 1994. And Her Writings Were Released By The Vatican In 1996. Still Many Do Not Know About Luisa.

Living In A Fallen Nature

We Have All Been Living In This Culture Of Death–

Most Humans Do Not Realize The Great Evil That Living In A Fallen State Does To Us Humans and To Our Entire Universe.

And We Are All Living In A Flood Of Sin and Death – And Most Pretend That This Is All Normal.

Just Because We Are Alive Right Now And Can Learn About This Gift Makes Us Blessed Beyond Our Imagination–

– If We Will Keep Learning About And Sign Ourself Over To Living In The Divine Will.

God Knew From All Eternity That We Would Be Living Right Now On Earth.

God Has Allowed Evil To Run Its Course In Us And In The World –

So That We Will Seek His Refuge, And Sign Ourselves Over To His Gift Of A New and Higher Divine Life.

And God Has allowed Everything That Has Happened in Your Life –

To Bring You Into The Forgiveness And Happiness Of The Divine Will.

How To Live In The Divine Will

We Must- In Our Heart Of Hearts- Feel Repugnance For Living In The Fallen Nature And In This Culture Of Death- And Turn To Jesus To Receive This Gift- Which Is the Fix and The Cure For All Our Problems-

But We Have To Learn About It And Truly Desire It- And Sign Ourselves Over To It- And Begin Living In It!

It's Simple And Easy To Do- To The Degree That We Are Willing To Make the Greatest Of

Sacrifices And Sign Ourselves Over To God Completely On His Specific Divine Will Terms.

We Call Jesus Into Doing All Our Acts With His Will, And Blessing All, And Giving A Return Of Love To The Father For All.

God Could Not Restore Human Beings And The Earth To Its Pristine Original State Of Holiness Because Mankind Was Not Interiorly Ready And Prepared To Accept God's Terms For This New And Higher Divine Life.

But Now We Are All Prepared And Interiorly Disposed Of We Will Accept God's Terms.

Why Now?

Luisa Asked Jesus, If This Gift Was So Great, then Why Didn't He Give It 2,000 Years Ago When He Was On Earth?

Jesus Replied That People Were Not Ready To Receive It.

He had To Give Us First The Redemption and Take Us From The Lesser To The Greater Knowledge And Interiorly Dispose Us To Receive A Gift And A Grace So Great.

So He Gave Us The Redemption, and Now The Gift Of The Divine Will– The Sanctification.

We Have All - Corporately - Been Exposed To The Church And The Bible and to The Sacraments And The Saints.

Humanity Has Grown In Our Knowledge Of God And Humanity Over The last 2,000 Years, And God Has Allowed Evil To Now Rain Upon The Earth;

And We See How Evil- Evil Is and Can Reject It; We All Have Broken Hearts - Broken Human Wills.

This Is Our Time Of Decision. Get In The Ark Of Refuge - The Living In The Divine Will- Or Stay Living In The Human Will Running Our Lives Outside Of The Divine Will – But Remember, Outside Of The Divine Will Be Gnashing Of Teeth.

This Refers To Our Human Will Being Frustrated And Tormented. But Living In he Divine Will Is All Happiness And Joy- Even If We Suffer.

Mathew 13:47-50 ESV

"Again, the Kingdom of Heaven is like a net that was thrown into the sea and gathered fish from every kind. When it was full, men drew it ashore and sat down and sorted the good into containers but threw away the bad.

So it will be at the End of the Age. The angels will come out and separate the evil from the righteous and throw them into the fiery furnace in that place there will be weeping and gnashing of teeth."

We Have A New Option On Earth Today!

If We Are Sick And Tired Of Being Sick And Tired, And We See The Gift That God Is Offering Us On Earth In The Gift Of The Divine Will- The Fortunate Few Will Say Yes.

Jesus Told Luisa That We Are To No Longer Seek The Suffering Of The Saints That Have Gone Before Us.

They Struggled To Conform Their Human Will To Do God's Will, But Now We Can Sign Over Our Human Will To God Taking Over Our Human Will And Running Our Life.

We Give God Full Rights Over Us-And Forget About Ourselves. We Sign Ourselves Over To God, As Victim Souls, Willing To Suffer And Die For Him, If That Is What He Wants.

We Give Him Our Human Will Completely– And Jesus Takes Over The Drivers Seat In Our Body And Soul.

We Just Get On Board For The Heavenly Ride.

Jesus Let's us Sit On His Lap, While He Drives.

All Our Past Struggles Are Over! When You Arrive At Living In The Divine Will You Have Done It All.

The Greatest Thing

Living In The Divine Will Is The Greatest Thing That We Can Do-

Here Is A Quote From The Book Of Heaven on Living In The Divine Will That Jesus Dictated To Luisa Piccarreta:

From The Book: I Bring You Tidings Of Great Joy (Luke 2,10) Third Edition Selection Of Passages About The Divine Will (A work of Pablo Martin – Civitavecchia 1992) (12)

BOOK OF HEAVEN – Volume 12, July 25, 1917

The Divine Will Instantly Purifies and Enriches the Soul in the Act of Entering Into the Divine Volition *"You must know that the most noble, most sublime, most grand, most heroic act is to do my Will and operate in my Volition.*

Therefore, no other act can equal this act. I make a display of all My Love and Generosity.

Scarcely does the soul decide to do it, then I give her the honor of holding her in My Volition, in that act in which the two volitions encounter each other to fuse themselves one in the other to form One alone. If she is stained, I purify her; if the thorns of human nature envelop her, I break them; and if some nail transfixes her, that is sin, I pulverize it because nothing of evil can enter into My Will.

Indeed, all My Attributes invest her and change weakness into strength, ignorance into knowledge, misery into riches and so with all the rest. And in the other acts there remains always something of one's self, but these acts are completely despoiled of one's self; and I fill her all with Me."

The Real Underlying Problem

Jesus Has Explained To Luisa That The Real Underlying Problem Is That Human Beings Are Living A Fallen Existence That Is Killing Us. This Living In A Fallen Existence Is Coming To An End.

Baptism Removes Original Sin, But Baptism does not remove the tendency to sin, which is called concupiscence.

We are born into a sinful state -with our human will in charge: and have two choices: to sin or sin.

Our Acts Are Tainted By Our Human Will Acting Outside The Full Enclosure Of The Divine Will.

That Is why there is The Sacrament of Penance- We Can Confess Our Sins.

But We Are Still Living With Our Human Will Disconnected From The Fullness Of The Divine Will.

And Now The Situation Is Made Worse: The Entire Earth Is Being Deluged And Is Drowning In A Culture Of Sin And Death!

A Fallen Nature – Means Our Human Nature Is Defective – From The Fall Of Adam and Eve Right Up To Today– That Is, Almost From The Beginning Of Our Creation– And We Have All Been Living Like That All Our History!

(Except Jesus And Mary– Who Lived In The Divine Will– And Now Luisa Piccarreta And All Those Living In The Gift Of The Divine Will.)

Jesus Came And Paid The Complete Price To Restore To Us Everything That Adam And Eve Lost.

So Why Is There Still Sin and Death? Because We Are Not Sanctified.

Why The Gift Now?

Luisa Asked Jesus, Why Didn't He Give Us The Gift Of The Divine Will 2,000 Years Ago When He Was On Earth?

Jesus Explained To Luisa That People Were Not Ready To Receive The Sanctification.

We Had To Be Taken From The Lesser To the Greater Knowledge Of God and Humanity and Be Prepared To Receive A Gift So Great.

He Could Only Give Us Salvation, But Not The Sanctification- That Is - To Be Made Holy.

The Specific Problem Is That Our Human Will Is Disconnected From God's Divine Will.

We Humans Were Designed And Created To Have Our Human Wills (Which Runs Our Souls) Connected To And Completely Operated By And

Directed By The Fullness Of God's Divine Will (This Is The Same Divine Will That Runs The Trinity.)

But It Takes Us To Learn About It, And Willing To Make The Greatest Of Sacrifices To Sign Over Our Human Will To The Operating Power Of The Divine Will In All Things.

Jesus Explained To Luisa Piccarreta The Problem With The State Of Humanity and Gave Her The Cure For Herself And For All Humanity.

The Problem: We Are Living In A "Fallen" Nature

The Cure: We Receive The Gift Of Living In The Divine Will.

This is The Only Problem That Exists Between God And Man: That Our Human Will Is Running Our Souls and Our Lives 'On Its Own' – Outside Of The Fullness Of The Divine Will.

THE TEST

The Following Quoted From Fr. Pablo Martin:

I Bring You Tidings Of Great Joy (Luke 2,10) 4th Edition (A work of Fr. Pablo Martin – Civitavecchia 1992)

Selection of Passages about the Divine Will taken from the writings of Luisa Piccarreta "The Little Daughter of the Divine Will" The Servant of God Luisa Piccarreta, Dominican Tertiary who died in the odor of sanctity at Corato, Bari, Italy on March 4th, 1947.

Fr. Pablo Martin: **"That is the problem: the only one in the end that exists: that of the relationship between the will of God and ours.**

Both were already represented in the two mysterious and symbolic plants of the terrestrial

paradise: **The Tree Of Life** and **The Tree Of The Knowledge Of Good And Evil.**

The Blessed Fruits of the First is Life, The First Fruit of The Second, of which man must not eat, Is Death.

The Divine Will descended for love in its work of Creation. It is present in each created thing in which it gives existence, energy and life, the life of its infinite qualities, by which the Heavens and the Earth are Full Of Its Glory.

Also in the man, Adam, created perfect and immaculate – the Divine Will was present and alive, so much more glorious for how much as man surpassed in dignity and beauty all other created beings.

The other beings, in fact are works, creatures of God; But the man, Adam was created in the capacity of son of God.

In Adam God established all other future men, all called to be sons of God. But Adam and all his progeny were invited to be sons of God on account of Jesus Christ, the Incarnate word, the first born among all creatures

(Col. 1,15-17) "the head of every man

(1 Cor. 11,3) "The Heir" of all creation

(Luke 20, 14). In Adam, son of God

(Luke 3,38). The Divine Will wanted to form not only his life, since Adam was made a "living soul"

(1 Cor. 15,45), but the very supernatural Life of God and was a gift of grace. For this, the Tree of Life was "in the middle of the garden" (Gen.2,9). (P.57)

<u>But it was necessary that the Gift be accepted freely and for love as God offered it freely and for love.</u>

<u>There is the precise significance of the test.</u>

Without the test, free and total acceptance of the Divine Will, God would have had servants, indeed, slaves but not sons, a thing unworthy of his Love.

<u>Man would have had his human will "as if he did not have it;" therefore, he would have had to sacrifice it, that is to consecrate it, which is to offer it in gift of love to God, to take in its place the Gift of the Divine Will."</u>

God's Basic Plan

Jesus Explained God's Basic Plan To Luisa Piccarreta.

Most Christians Do Not Understand God's Basic Plan Laid Out In The Bible:

God Spent 4,000 Years Of The Old Testament Times To Prepare Humanity To Receive Jesus Christ And The Redemption and The Gifts Of Salvation, And 2,000 More Years To Prepare Humanity To Receive The Gift Of The Divine Will– The Sanctification.

There Are Three Comings Of Jesus:

FIRST, In The Redemption.

SECOND, In The Middle Coming, For the Sanctification. – Happening Now,

(This Is the Silent Spiritual Coming Of Jesus Into Believers To Prepare The Bride For The Wedding Feast Of The Era Of Peace,)

THIRD, Is The Definitive Second Coming For The Final Judgement. At The End of The Millennium Of Peace/The Era Of Peace –

In Gods Basic Plan– Many Christians Forget The Sanctification And The Era Of Peace.

In The Redemption Jesus Paid The Full Price – And Jesus Gave The Gifts Of Salvation – The Church And The Sacraments And Over A Period Of The Last 2,000 Years, With The Devotions, And The Bible, And The Lives Of The Saints Who Are Our Modern Day Prophets.

And Now In Our Time – With Luisa Piccarreta And The Gift Of Living In the Divine Will:

And This Ushers In The Millennium Of Peace —

The Era Of Peace For The World.

And Then At The End Of The Era Of Peace - Satan Will Be Released For A Short Time And Jesus Comes In The Definitive Second Coming, And It's The Final Judgement And It Is Heaven Or Hell For Eternity.

The Gift Of Living In The Divine Will Is The Spiritual Indwelling Of The Trinity <u>And The Operational Control Of The Fullness Of The Divine Will That Runs The Trinity.</u>

This is The Kingdom Of God Coming To Live In Us Completely.

If We Don't Take This Gift Of Divine Refuge, We Risk Being Overcome In The Purification That Is Taking Place.

The Greatest Purification

This is The Greatest Purification That Has Ever Happened On Earth, And Is By Divine Decree!

This Is The Great Tribulation that The Bible Told Us About.

This Is Not The Final Judgement That Only Comes In The Definitive Second Coming That Occurs At The End Of The Era Of Peace, But Jesus Tells Us That "Most Of This Generation Will Be Destroyed" In This Tribulation And Chastisement.

Many Call It "A Judgement In Miniature," with Magor Cataclysmic Events. The Whole Earth Will Be Literally Shaken And Transformed. The Purification Has Started And Will Not End Until Most Of This Generation Is Destroyed And The Era Of Peace Comes Upon The Whole Earth.

This Chastisement May Be Lessened, But This Chastisement Is By Divine Decree.

It is Man Rising Up Against Man, Nature Rising Up Against Man, And God's Chastisements From Heaven – All Because Man Is Out Of The Will Of God.

The Divine Will Is Our Refuge, And Our Sanctification, And Our New And A New Higher Divine Life For Us – and To Prepare The World For The Era Of Peace That Is God's Plan For The Entire World: A New Start For Humanity.

From The Booklet: I Bring You Tidings Of Great Joy – (Luke 2:10)

Selections of Passages about the Divine Will, taken from the writings of the Servant of God Luisa Piccarreta, "The Little Daughter of the Divine Will." (A Work Of Father Pablo Martin, Civitavecchia 1992)

Jesus Dictated The Following Message To Luisa Piccarreta (1865-1947)

The Fatherly Appeal With His Father and The Holy Spirit

The Divine King appeals to His children on earth to come now and enter into the Kingdom Of His Will –

"My Dear And Beloved Children, I come into your midst with My Heart all drowned in flames of love, I come as a Father to be among My children because I love you so very much.

My Love is so great that I come to remain with you so that we may live together with one single Will; with one single Love...As I come to you, I bring with me My pains, My Blood, My Works, and even My very Death. ... Even my death wants to give rebirth to the Life of My Will in you. "... I have prepared everything for you in My Humanity, and

I have prepared for and obtained graces, helps, light and strength for you to receive a Gift so great.

On my part I have done everything; so now I am waiting for you to do your part. Who would be so ungrateful as to turn Me away and not welcome the Gift that I am bringing to you?"

"Know that My Love is so much that I will forget about your past life, your sins, all your evil; And I will bury them in the ocean of my Love to burn them all away; And then we will begin a new life together, all of My Will."

"Who would have the heart to refuse Me and send Me away without accepting My visit which is so full of a Father's Love? But, if you will welcome Me, I will remain with you as a Father in the midst of his children. **Then we must be in the greatest accord and live together with one Will alone.**

Oh, how much I long for this; how I moan, how I

cry, even going into delirium, and weeping because **I want My dearest children to gather around Me and live with My very Own Will**"

... "I come as King to live among his people, but not for the purpose of levying taxes and heaping burdens upon you. No. No. I come because I want your will, your miseries, your weaknesses, all your evils."

[He Is Taking Away Everything That Distresses Us]

"My sovereignty is really this: I want everything that distresses you and causes you to be unhappy and restless so that I can hide it within My Love and burn it all away. As beneficent pacific, and magnanimous King that I am, I want to exchange My Will for yours, filling you with my most tender Love, with My Riches, and Happiness, with My Peace and most pure Joy."

[All We Have To Do Is To Give Him Our Human Will And Take On His Will]

"If you will give me your will all will be done just as I have said; And you will make Me happy, and you will be happy too. I long for nothing else than for my Will to reign among you ..." (Words which Jesus gives to His children through Luisa Piccarreta, 1925)

It's a Purification

We Are Living In The Time Of The Greatest Purification - Chastisement That The Earth Has Ever Known, In Which Most Of Humanity Will Be Destroyed.

It's A Purification - Like The Purification Of The Earth At The Time Of Noah And The Great Flood.

Jesus Tells Luisa That The Survivors Will Be Few, But Will Live In A Renewed Earth.

It Is The Biblically Promised Millennium Of Peace.

-No More Sickness And No More Death. -Some Will Live 1,000 Years.

-The Earth Will Be Joined To Paradise.   -The Kingdom Comes, And The Demon Is Cast Out.

Jesus Explains The Times

Book Of Heaven Quote Of Jesus To Luisa

"My beloved daughter, I want you to know the order of my Providence."

Volume 12 – January 29, 1919

"My beloved daughter, I want you to know the order of my Providence.

In every 2,000– year period I have renewed the world.

In the first period I renewed it with the Flood. In the second 2,000 years, I renewed it with my coming to the earth and manifesting my Humanity from which, as so many channels of light, my Divinity shone.

And in this third period of 2000 years, those who are good, and the Saints themselves have lived the fruit of my humanity, but have enjoyed my Divinity scarcely at all.

"Now we are at the end of the third period and there will be a third renovation. This is why there is general confusion. It is due to the preparation for the third renovation. And if in the second renovation I have manifested what my Humanity did and suffered, little was said about the working of my Divinity.

Now in this third renovation, after the purging of the earth and the destruction of a large part of the present generation, I will be still more generous with creatures.

I will complete the renovation by manifesting what my Divinity did in my humanity, how my Divine Will worked with my Human Will, how everything remained joined in Me, how I did and redid everything, and even the thoughts of each creature were redone by me and sealed with my Divine Will.

My Love wishes to release itself and make known the excesses that my Divinity worked in my Humanity for creatures.

Of My Will, the grace, the enchantment and sweetness that it contains. But to penetrate within, to embrace its immensity, to multiply oneself with Me, to penetrate everywhere, even while on earth, to penetrate into Heaven and into Hearts, to abandon human ways and work with Divine ways... This is yet this is not yet known.

And this is so true that it will appear strange to many, and whoever does not have his mind open to the light of the truth will understand nothing.

But little by little, I will make my way, manifesting at different times truths about my Will in such manner that they will finally understand.

These excesses greatly surpassed those which my humanity visibly worked. This is why I often speak to you about living in My Will which I have not manifested to anyone until now.

Two Generations

Jesus Told Luisa That He Has Two Generations Within Himself-

And He Calls The Generation That We Have Been Living For All Of Human Existence- "The Generation Of Darkness" and Those Who Are Entering Into The Living In The Divine Will Are "The Second Generation Of the Children Of Light."

We Have Been Living In "The Generation Of Darkness-"

All Of Human History- Since Adam And Eve Fell And Changed The State Of The Nature Of Human Beings To A Fallen Nature-

Which Weakened Our Whole Body And Soul- And All Of The Universe!

Our Intellect Is Dimmed, Our Memory Is Faulty, And Our Will Is Disconnected From God's Will Which Is Intended To Be Running Our Life.

In The Gift Of The Divine Will, He Is Raising Up A Whole New Generation Of Human Beings On Earth Right Now –

Transforming People From Fallen Human Beings– "The Generation Of Darkness." Into "The Second Generation Of The Children Of Light" To Populate The New Era Of Peace Coming To The Whole Earth,

After The Purification And The Great Tribulation That Will Destroy Most Of This Generation– And Most Of This Earth– God Will Be More Generous With The Survivors.

Book Of Heaven –

Volume 14 – October 27, 1922

The Divine Will: Inheritance Of Jesus For The Creatures. Two Generations.

Luisa: "

I was thinking to myself about all that has been written in these past days, and I thought to myself: How is it possible that my sweet Jesus has waited for so long to make known all that His humanity operated in the Divine Will for love of creatures?

But while I was thinking of this, my always lovable Jesus, making Himself seen with His Heart opened, told me: "Daughter of My Will, why concern yourself? This happened also in Creation. How long did I not keep It in my womb as really formed? And when I pleased, I put it out. And even Redemption, How long did I not keep It within me? I could say from eternity; yet, I waited much time before descending from Heaven and bringing

It to fulfillment, this is my usual way: first I fecundate my work, I form them within Myself, and at the appropriate time I put them out.

Even more, you must know that my Humanity contained two generations within itself: the children of darkness and the children of light.

I came to rescue the former, and so I gave out my Blood in order to save them. My Humanity was holy, and nothing did It inherent of the miseries of the first man; and although it was similar in natural features, it was untouchable to the slightest spot which could shade my sanctity.

My only inheritance was the Will of my Father, in which I was to carry out all of my human acts, to form in me the generation of the children of light.

You see, I was allowed to form this generation in the very womb of the Will of my Celestial Father, and I spared no toils, no acts, nor pains, nor prayers; on the contrary, it was at the top of all the things I did and suffered, in such a way that I conceived it in me, I fecundated it and I formed it.

They were the ones whom the Divine Father had entrusted to Me with so much love; they were my beloved inheritance, which was given to Me in the Most Holy Supreme Will.

Now, after I have made known the goods of Redemption and how I want everyone to be saved, giving to all the means which are needed,

I move on to make known that there is another generation in me, which I must deliver; My children who will live in the Divine Will;

And that in my own Heart I keep all the graces prepared- all my interior acts done in the sphere of Eternal Will for them-

waiting for the kiss of their acts, for their union, in order to give them the inheritance of the Supreme Will."

The Promised Time

Our Time IS The Promised Time–
The Wheat and the Chaff Are Being Separated.
We All Need To Get In The Ark Of Our Lady

Which Is Our Refuge For This Time.

We Are In The Birth Pangs Of Major Cataclysmic
Events
That Will Fall On The Good and The Bad,
And That Will Destroy Most Of Humanity
And Most Of This Civilization.

The Destruction Of This Generation And Of This
Civilization Has Started!

It Is Man Rising Up Against Man, Nature Rising
Up Against Man, and God's Chastisements Of Fire
From Heaven.

If You Are In The Refuge Of The Divine Will – And
You Die You Will Go To The Highest Place In

Heaven –

And The Survivors Who Live In The Divine Will –
Will Live In The Era Of Peace – Upon The Earth –
The Millennium Of Peace Promised In The Bible.

What Is This Gift?

This is The Kingdom Of God Descending From
Heaven To Earth In Us.
It Is A Divine Possession– Meaning God Is Coming
Down From Heaven And Living In Us –

This Has Never Been Available To Fallen Human
Beings And Is God Taking Over Control Of Our Life
And Raising Us Up To A Higher Divine Life.

How Do We Receive This Gift?

You Simply Give The Consent Of Your Will To
Allowing God To Take Over Running Your Life and
To Sanctify You–

To Make You Holy–
Once You Know What This Gift Is– You Must
Desire It – Even Willing To Sacrifice Your Life.

This Is An All Or None Covenant. And Jesus
Takes You At Your Word And Takes Over Control Of
Your Life.

Jesus Explained To Luisa - How God Lives In Us:

*God's Will Connects Our Human Will Back Up To
Gods Divine Will, And God Pours His Divine Will Into
Our Soul and God Lives In Our Acts.*

*As St. Augustine Teaches That God Will Not Save Us
Without Our Cooperation.*

We Pray: Jesus You Do It In Me. Pray In My Praying. Think In My Thinking. Walk In My Walking, etc. – for every act that we do.

Once You Enter Into The Gift Of Living In The Divine Will,

In Every Act You Receive All the Graces Of All the Sacraments Ever Given, And More!
You Receive Perfect Union With God. The Gift Of The Divine Will Is God Giving Himself Completely To Us, And We Give Ourselves Completely To God.

Be Careful With This Gift.
When You Enter Into The Divine Will, You Enter Into The Sinless Ark Of The Blessed Virgin Mary, the Sinless Ark Of the Covenant.

We Are being Lifted Up Above the Mud And Evil Of the World and Will Be Set Down In the Era Of Peace

Upon the Earth – On The Seventh Day – the Day Of Rest.

King David Was Bringing The Ark Of The Covenant To Jerusalem.
And You Remember What Happened To Uzzah In the Old Testament When He Unworthily Touched The Ark Of the Covenant – That Foretold The Sinless Ark Of The Covenant –Which Is The Blessed Virgin Mary?

Uzzah Was Struck Dead For Unworthily Touching the Ark.

Now, You Already Know Enough To Say Yes To This Gift;

You Just Sign Over All Your Life Over To Jesus – and He Takes Over Complete Control Of Your

Life – And You Live A New And Higher Divine Existence!

You Give Your Yes, And You Keep Learning, and Signing Yourself Over To Living In This Gift.

But Be Aware!
God Will Sanctify You and Strip You Of All Attachments in The Human Will.

This Involves A Lot Of Suffering, But It's Jesus Suffering In You. And We Make A Return Of Love To The Father In All Our Acts.

YOU HAVE A NEW AND HIGHER DIVINE LIFE!
YOU JUST HAVE TO KEEP LEARNING ABOUT
THE GIFT OF THE DIVINE WILL,
AND TO KEEP SIGNING YOURSELF OVER TO IT,
AND YOU WILL ENTER IN DEEPER AND DEEPER
ON EARTH,

AND THEN LIVE IN THE DIVINE WILL IN HEAVEN FOR ETERNITY.

The Knowledge Of The Divine Will Is The Army Of Light, And Us Doing Our Acts- In The Divine Will Are The Ammunition of Light.

You have to read and study The Book Of Heaven And Call Jesus Into Doing Your Acts In the Divine Will.

And As You Call Jesus Into Doing All Your Acts In The Divine Will, The Divine Will Is Pulsed Into You From The Center Of The Trinity- and This Power Goes Out To All and Back To The Father. This Is How the Human Will Is Defeated, And The Divine Will Triumphs!

Do Not Wait For The Era Of Peace To Come - Because the Era Of Peace is Being Formed In Those Who Are Taking Up Living In The Gift Of The

Divine Will.

 This is The Quickest, Fastest, And Most Effective Way To Become Holy, But It Is Still A Process, and You Must Be Disposed To Make The Greatest Of Sacrifices, Unto Death.

In Union

This Gift is In Union – One With The Catholic Church

I Am Not A Theologian, So The Following Section Is To Give You A Very Basic Understanding Of What We Receive In The Gift Of The Divine Will Versus The Eucharist– It Is The Same Presence.

We Are Not Absolved From Living All The Rules Of The Church.

There Is No Change Exteriorly.

The Divine Will Enhances All The Sacraments And Devotions Of The Church.

This Gift Is Perfect Interior Disposition To Receive The Sacraments. We Know That The Sacraments Are Only Effective To The Degree That We Are Interiorly Disposed To Receive Them.

In The Gift Of Living In The Divine Will We Receive The Divine Will Which Contains All Of God and His Attributes. The Real Presence Of Jesus Lives Perennially In Us.

We Become Living Hosts Of The Living God. The Living In The Divine Will Is Perennial Communion.

The Living In The Divine Will May Also Be For A Time When The Sacraments Are Not Available And We Can Still Have Union With God.

Now, Jesus Told Luisa that The Living In The Divine Will Is Greater Than The Sacraments.

With One Act In The Divine Will, You Receive All The Graces Of All The Sacraments Ever Given, And More! You Receive Perennial Communion With God. Jesus Asked Luisa, What Gave The Sacraments? And He Answered Her: The Divine Will.

In the Divine Will We become Living Hosts Which Brings Glory To God With The Same Real Presence Of God That Lives In The Eucharist.

But In The Eucharist, The Real Presence Of Jesus Stays Only Approximately 15 Minutes after we take Communion.

"The Eucharistic presence of Christ begins at the moment of the consecration and endures as long as the Eucharistic Species subsist" (The Catholic Catechism- CCC 1377).

In The Living In The Divine Will, We Receive The Divine Presence As Well -But Living In Our Soul And In Our Acts.

Book Of Heaven

Volume 9 – March 23, 1910

Living In The Divine Will Is Greater Than Communion

Luisa Speaking:

As I was in my usual state, and lamenting because of His privations, He came just in passing and told me: "My daughter, I recommend that you not get out of my Will, because my Will contains such power as to be a new Baptism for the soul- and even more than Baptism itself.

In fact while in the Sacraments there is part of my Grace, in my Will there is the whole fullness of it.

In the Baptism, the stain of original sin is removed, but passions and weaknesses remain. In my Will since the soul destroys her own volition, she also destroys passions, weaknesses and all that is human; and she lives of the virtues, of the fortitude and of all the Divine qualities."

On hearing this, I said to myself: 'In a little while He is going to say that His Will is greater than Communion Itself.'

And He added: "Of course, of course, because the Sacramental Communion lasts a few minutes, while my Will is perennial communion; even more, eternal– entering eternity in Heaven.

The Sacramental Communion is subject to some obstacles, either because of illness, or necessity, or because of those who have to administer It; while the Communion of my Will is not subject to any hindrance. If the soul only wants it, all is done.

No one can prevent her from having such a great good which forms the happiness of the earth and of Heaven – neither demons, nor creatures, and not even the Omnipotence Itself. **The soul is free; no one has any right over her at this point of my Will.** This is why I push It, and I want so much that creatures take It: It is the most important thing for Me; the thing which I cherish the most."…

The Gift Of Living In The Divine Will Is A Divine
Possession.

*We Sign Ourself Over To God Living In Us, And He
Does All Our Actions.*
God Lives In Our Actions.

luisapiccarreta.com Book Of Heaven– Volume 11–
August 20, 1913

*We Form Divine Lives Of Jesus As Jesus Does Our
Acts. How The Divine Will will form many Jesuses
where It Reigns.*

*One who lives in the Divine Will must have trust,
simplicity and disinterest in giving to all. Her life and
her work are ended, because the Divine Will
consecrates her and transubstantiates her.*

Luisa: While I was praying, I saw my always adorable Jesus within me, and many souls around me, who were saying: **'Lord, You have placed everything in this soul!** 'And stretching their hands toward me, they said: 'Since Jesus is in you, and all His goods are with Him, take them and give them to us.' I remain confused and blessed

Jesus told me: "My daughter (Luisa), all possible goods are contained in my Will, and it is necessary for the soul who lives in It to be in It with trust, operating as owner together with Me.

Creatures expect everything from this soul, and if they don't receive it, they feel defrauded. But how can she give if she does not operate together with me in complete confidence?

Therefore, trust in giving; simplicity in communicating herself to all; disinterest for herself, to be able to live completely for Me and for her neighbor are necessary for the soul who lives in my Will. Such am I.

Then He added: "My daughter (Luisa), It happens to one who does my Will as to a grafted tree: the power of the graft has the virtue of destroying the life of the tree which receives the graft. Therefore, one can no longer see the fruits and the leaves of the first tree, but those of the graft. And if the first tree said to the graft: 'I Want to keep at least a little branch, so that I too will be able to get some fruits from me in order to make everybody know that I still exist', The graft would say: 'You have no more reason to exist after you submitted yourself to receive my graft. Life will be all mine.'

In the same way, the soul who does my Will can say: 'My life is ended. I will no longer produce my works, my thoughts, my words, but the works, thoughts and words of the One whose Will is my Life.'

Therefore, I say to the one who does my Will: 'You are my life my blood, my bones, ..."

The true, real, sacramental transformation takes place, not by virtue of the words of the Priest, but by virtue of my Will.

As soon as the soul decides to live in my Volition, my Will creates Myself within the soul; And as My Will flows in the will, works and steps of the soul, she undergoes as many of my creations.

It happens just as to a pyx full of consecrated particles: There are as many Jesuses as many particles– one for each particle. In the same way, by virtue of my Will, the soul contains Myself in her whole being, as well as in each particle of it. One who does my Will fulfills the true eternal Communion–a Communion with complete fruit."

A Basic Understanding Of The Gift

My Goal Is To Provide A Basic Understanding Of The Gift Of The Divine Will – To Give You A Very Basic Structure And Point The Way To The Writings Of Luisa Piccarreta.

In This Book I Am Reporting Some Basics Of What The Writings Of Luisa Piccarreta Tell Us:

About The Gift Of The Divine Will Now Available To Everyone,
And The Times We Live In.

The Divine Will Is A Free Gift,
But The Knowledge Of This Gift Is Preeminent.

It Is The Fulfillment Of The New Covenant –
And We Have To Know What It Is, So that We Know How To Sign Ourselves Over To It, And Live In It.

We Have To Know How It Works, So That We Can Desire, And Receive, And Live In This Gift.

There is Divine Power In Every Word Of "The Book Of Heaven" Dictated By Jesus To Luisa Piccarreta.

If You Don't Know What This Gift Is, Then You Cannot Desire It, Or Love It, Or Live In It.

Jesus Appeared To Luisa Piccarreta – and Dictated 36 Volumes Of Instructions On How To Live In The Divine Will.

Jesus Explained To Luisa What The Problem With The Human Condition Is, And How To Live In It. Jesus Explained How God Created Adam And Eve In The Image And Likeness Of God, With The Divine Will Possessing And Diffused In Our Human Will. Jesus Wants Us To See The Problem With The Human Condition Which Is The Only Problem That Exists Between God And Man.

There Is Divine Power In Every Word of "The Book Of Heaven"

Book Of Heaven – August 25,1921

... The more knowledge one has about the Divine Will, the more value his acts acquire."

"The Book Of Heaven" is God's Instruction Book On How To Live In The Divine Will.

A New Garden Of Eden

A New Garden Of Eden Is Coming To The Entire World. This Is The Biblical Millennium Of Peace.

We Are Witness To What It Feels Like To Live At The End Of A Civilization and The Transition To A Greater One, Which Is The "Big **Event**" That All Humanity Is Awaiting.

The First Generation Of Human Beings Is Coming To An End. And The Way Of Life That We Have Been Living Is Coming To An End.

Human Beings Were Created And Started Out In The Mists Of The Garden Of Eden, As the Garden Of Delights.

But After The Fall, This Became The "Empire Of Darkness" That We Are Living In –

And Is Dying Out In Bursts Of The Fire Of War And Transgression Of God's Laws, Of Diseases,

Forest Fires, and Volcanos, And Pollution And Dry Rivers.

It's Nature Rising Up Against Man, And Man Rising Up Against Man, And God's Chastisements Of Fire From Heaven. And It's All Because Man Is Out Of The Will Of God.

We Are The Witnesses To The Fall Of This 6,000-YEAR Civilization.

"The Empire Of Darkness" Is The Greatest And Longest Epic In History Lasting From Adam And Eve Until Its Last Vestiges – Which We Are Now Witnessing-

The Fall Of "The Empire Of Darkness" Is What We See And Smell All Around Us, In The Smell Of Marijuana Lingering In Wasted City Streets Littered With The Homeless, and Hopeless.

But The Most Telling Sign Of The Sad Ending Of This Civilization Is: The Apathy Of Most

People On Earth, Especially Those Who Consider Themselves "Comfortable."

The Human Will Is Running Amuck, And For The Most Part Is Not Seeking A Cure.

Most People Are All Wrapped Up In Their Own Problems And Concerns, And Don't Want To Know What God Is Offering Us.

Satan Appears To Be Powerful- And Ready To Claim Victory- But Satan Is Inflated Like A Huge Parade Clown Balloon- And Is Imploding!

Man Is Out Of Energy Because He Is Out Of God's Will –Nature Is Out Of Balance And Attacking Man And This Godless Civilization –

Jesus Told Luisa that The Most Certain Sign That The New Era Of Peace Is Coming Upon the World After The Destruction Of Most Of Humanity –

Is That He Has Communicated This Great Gift
Of The Divine Will To Luisa Piccarreta–

**God Has Not Abandoned Us, And He Has Given
Us – For This Moment We Are Living – Right Now
On Earth– The Greatest Gift That He Could Ever
Give Us– Even In Heaven.**

Our Lady Of Walsingham

The Era of the Kingdom of the Divine Will on Earth

The Community Of Our Lady Of Walsingham – website

"The Gift of The Divine Will which God now wishes to give to the world is not only about doing God's will but possessing God's will, i.e.., letting God carry out his own will, Himself, within us through our consent.

This is what Adam was doing up until the Fall, and what Jesus did in His Humanity throughout his whole life while here on Earth.

Jesus points out that Luisa, who received the Gift Of The Divine Will on 8th September 1889, marks the beginning of the era of the Kingdom of the Divine Will on earth. This gift is now available to everyone."

For more information on this please visit the
following site: http://luisapiccarreta.com

Divine Will Life

divinewilllife.org

Fr. Robert Young

November 13, 2010 – V12, Week 4

From The Recording: "What does living in the Divine Will mean?

All of our lives– every moment, every thought, word, and deed is done with His Divine Will as the operating power and force and love in our lives; and so that's what he wants for us now and this is really how we understand the **Kingdom** reigning on earth as in Heaven.

How can it possibly reign here, as it reigns in Heaven? When we see all the evil in the world – we see all the lack of cooperation with God's Will by the human will.

Well it can happen when a soul - any soul through the inspiration of God and through the Holy Spirit and God's Grace comes to know that it's possible in the Divine Will.

<u>And comes to desire it, and comes to choose to decide to live to receive that Gift, and then to live every moment in it. That's the way it happens - and so our human will is very much a part of this."</u>

A New Life

We Are Being Given A New And Higher Divine Way Of Living

God Is Coming To Live In Us and Take Over Control Of Our Lives!

This is The Crux Of The Situation Humanity Is In:

Will We Learn about The Gift And Then Sign Ourselves Over To God Taking **Absolute** Control Of Our Lives In His Divine Will.

If God Is Running Our Lives, then What Problems Could We Have?

Whatever Is Going On, God Is Taking Care Of It!

Jesus explained to Luisa that this Gift is not new,

but what can be considered new is that it is A New Way Of Living To Us On Earth.

All Of Human History And The Universe Is Prelude And Has Built Up To God Giving This Gift Back To Humans.

Jesus Is The Messiah. And The Messiah Came To Redeem Us– To Pay Our Ransom, And To Restore Us Back To The Way We Were Living In Garden Of Eden.

The Garden Of Eden Is Being Formed In Those Living In The Divine Will– And Will Culminate In A New Garden Of Eden Coming To The Entire World.

This Is The Biblical Millennium Of Peace.

Jesus Paid Our Ransom In Full, For Us To Receive This Gift Of The Messiah.

Did You Ever Wonder, If Jesus Came To Restore The Kingdom To Humanity And The Earth, Then Why Is There Still Sin And Death?

First The Redemption And Then The Sanctification Which Is Happening Now In The Gift Of The Divine Will.

God Has Spent All Of Human History To Prepare This Gift Of The Divine Will- But Most **People** Are Not Following God's Stream Of Things.

Most Are Apathetic, Living In Their Fallen State –With Their Human Will Running Their Lives – And Totally Self- Oriented And Totally Oblivious.

They Don't Even Know That They Need To Be Healed And Placed Back On The Potters Wheel And Be Refashioned And Recreated In The Image And Likeness Of God. **This Means Everyone Of Us.**

We Are All Living In a Fallen Nature, and Everyone We Meet Is Living This Way. There's No Joy In Mudville, And Each Has the Secret Passions Of The Human Will.

This Apathy Is A Testament To Why God Has Intervened In Human History In Our Time- And the Chastisements That Have Begun.

THE PROBLEM WITH THE HUMAN CONDITION

Jesus Appeared To Luisa Piccarreta (1865-1947), The Greatest Saint And Prophet Of Our Time, And Explained To Her What The Problem With The Human Condition Is, And Gave Her The Cure.

The Problem Is That We Are Living In A Fallen State —For All Of Our Existence Since Adam and Eve – Our First Parents. We Are Unplugged From The Divine Will.

We Are Dim Bulbs.

Our Intellects Are Dimmed, Our Memories Are Faulty, And Our Will Is Weakened And Selfish.

Our Human Will Is Running Our Lives And Is Defective And Has Become More And More Deranged Over This Whole Generation Of Known Human History!

Do You Want To Be Healed?

Can You Imagine Asking A Fallen Human Being, That Is Defective In His Human Nature –But Feels Comfortable In their Life Style and In Their Human Will: Do You Want To Be Healed?

God Lives In Our Acts

You Must Know God Lives In Our Souls and in our Actions, That Is, Our Acts: What We Think, What We Do, In All Our Mental, Emotional, Physical Activities.

In Our Thoughts, Heartbeats, Breaths.

The Three Faculties, Or Powers Of Our Soul Are Our Intellect, Memory, And Will. Our Will Is The Primary Faculty.

Book Of Heaven – February 22, 1921

The Third Fiat will give such grace to the creature as to make him return almost to the state of origin; then,

God will take his perpetual rest in the last Fiat.

"In creating man, I endowed him with three powers– intellect, memory and will; and with the

three Fiats will I accomplish the work of the sanctification of man.”

“At the Creating Fiat, the intellect of man remains as though enraptured.”

“...In the Fiat of Redemption, his memory remains as though enchanted by the excesses of my love and suffering so much in order to help and save man in the state of sin.

“...In the Third Fiat, my love wants to display even more. I want to assail the human will;

I want to place My Own Will as support of his will, so that the human will may remain not only in rapture and enchanted, but sustained by an Eternal Will.

And as my Will becomes his support in everything, man will almost be unable to escape it.

The generations will not end until My Will reigns upon the earth.

"This Gift Is Divine Life."

Sun Of My Will

And So This Is The Crux Of The Human Story:

The Human Will– Is In Operational Control Of Our Human Life.

The Divine Will Is In Operational Control Of God's Divine Life.

*All Humans Were Designed And Created– To **Have Our Human Will Completely Fused To And Overseen And Directed By The Same Divine Will That Runs The Trinity.***

The Problem Is That Adam and Eve Pulled Their Human Will, out of The Operational Control Of The Divine Will – Which Is Intended To Run Our Human Life.

The Cure Is That We Sign Ourselves Over To God's Divine Will– Again Running Our Human Will And Our Lives.

The Blessed Virgin Best Explains This In Luisa's Book **"The Virgin Mary In The Kingdom Of The Divine Will."**, p.22.

"The creature, with its human will, is all vacillating, weak, inconstant disordered.

And this is so because God, in creating It, <u>created it united as in nature with His Divine Will</u> in such a way that it should be the strength, the prime movement, the support, the food, the life of the human will.

<u>Thus, by not giving life to the Divine Will in ours,</u> the goods received from God in Creation are rejected and also the rights received in nature in the act in which we were created."

The Real Problem

Thus the problem with the human condition is not that the human will is running our lives, but that we are disconnected from God's Divine Will Overseeing And Directing Our Human Will

In fact The Human Will Running Our Soul Is What Most Makes Us Most Like God.

Thus, All Those Who Live In This Gift Are All Living With The Same Heart – The Same Will- Which is God's Heart And His Will and We All Live In Perfect Harmony.

God Is Passing Out New Hearts- His Own Divine Will. The Divine Will is the Divine Power Being Poured Out Into Mankind! This Is The Gift That Adam And Eve Lost. Jesus And Mary Lived In The Divine Will.

A Proclamation

A Proclamation Of Great Favor To All The Earth:

By Divine Decree:

In The Midst Of The Darkness Of Evil Covering The Earth–

A New Day Is Dawning.

Jesus Appeared to a woman Luisa Piccarreta (1865-1947) Of Corato, Italy, and Gave Her The Biblically Promised Gift For Our Time:

The Gift Of Living In The Divine Will For Her And For All Humanity; And Explained To Her the Times That We Are Living In.

What Did Jesus Tell Luisa?

Jesus Told Luisa And Us Of The Times In Which We Live– And Gave Her The Greatest Gift That God Could Ever Give To Creatures–

This Is The Gift That Adam And Eve Had In The Garden Of Eden – Before Their Sin Of Disobedience–

And This Gift Has Been Given Back To Luisa For Her And For All Humans–

We Just have to learn about it, receive it, and live in it.

Your True Strength

If You Want To Find Your True Strength Given By The Power Of Christ Living Within – Then Take This Gift Of Living In The Divine Will!

THE GIFT OF LIVING IN THE DIVINE WILL IS A NEW AND DIVINE WAY TO LIVE.

You Live In The Heart Of God- Which Is The Divine Will. And God Lives In Our Heart-Our Will.

The Only Way

The Only Way In Is To Know This Gift Of Living In The Divine Will- Is To Receive It- ON GODS TERMS – AND LIVE IN IT.

YOU MUST READ THE INSTRUCTION MANUAL – *THE BOOK OF HEAVEN* THAT JESUS DICTATED TO LUISA, OR YOU DON'T KNOW What This Gift Is And How To Receive It And Live In It.

A New Heart

We Live In The Time Of The Fulfillment Of The New Covenant:

(Ezekiel 36: 26-30 KJV)

"A New Heart also will I give you, and A New Spirit will I put within you; and I will take away the Stony Heart out of your flesh, and I will give you an Heart Of Flesh.

And I will put My Spirit within you, and cause you to walk in My Statutes, and ye shall keep My judgments, and do them. And ye shall dwell in The Land that I gave to your father's; and ye shall be my people, and I will be your God.

And I will also save you from all your uncleannesses: and I will call for the corn, and will increase it, and lay no famine upon you. And I will multiply the fruit of the tree, and the increase of the field, that ye shall receive no more reproach of famine among the heathen.

The Light is Coming On Inside Of Us – For Those In The Divine Will.

This Gift Is The Interior Life Of God Coming Into Our Interior Life.

The Message Of Jesus To Humanity Right Now Is That Our Human Will Is Failing Us.

Our Human Will Is What Directs Our Life.

It Is The Operational Center Of Our Life.

Here is a key concept of the Divine Will:

In the Bible and The Writings of Luisa Piccarreta - in The Book Of Heaven:

240

The Redemption was to get us ready to receive "The Sanctification" which is what the Gift Of Living In The Divine Will is.

This Is The Most Blessed Time To Ever Be Alive

This is A More Blessed Time To Be Alive Than Even When Jesus Was Walking the Earth,

Because The Gift Of The Divine Will Has Now Been Given to Humanity and Is Available To Everyone Now Living– If You Learn About It And Receive It, And Live In It.

This Is The Sanctification Of Humanity.

Jesus Himself Explains To Luisa that When He Was On The Earth 2,000 Years Ago, He Could Not Give This Gift Because Humanity Was Not Ready To Receive The Gift.

Everything God Has Done Has Been To Prepare Us To Receive This Gift.

Everything God Did In The Redemption and Then Over The Past 2,000 Years Has Been To Give Us The Gift Of the Divine Will.

All The Church And The Sacraments And The Councils And The Apparitions And The Saints Have Been To Prepare Us To Receive This Gift.

He Came To Redeem, So That He Could Dispose Us To Receive A Gift So Great, And Return, And *Give* The Gift Of The Divine Will.

The Divine Will Was Second To The Redemption In Execution, But First In Intention.

The Most Blessed Time

In spite Of The Worldwide Conditions Of Sin And Death Raining Down Upon The Earth, *This Is Still The Most Blessed Time To Ever Be Alive Because The Gift Of The Divine Will Has Been Given To Humanity.*

Keep This In Mind Always And Learn To And Continuously Place Yourself In The Divine Will. This Is Our Happiness Right now On Earth And For Eternity In Heaven.

It Is Not The End Of The World, But The End Of An Era, And a Transition Into A Greater And More Magnificent Era For All Mankind On Earth.

This Message Is For The Whole World.
We Who Are Living Right Now Are The Most
Blessed Human Beings That Have Ever Lived On
Earth!

God Knew From All Eternity That We Would Be Living Right Now On Earth, And That This Gift Would Be Made Known To Us.

But Remember, To Be Divinely Blessed With This Gift, You Have To Learn About, Receive It, And Live In the Gift Of The Divine Will.

What Is The Gift?

It's a Divine Indwelling Never Before Given To Fallen Creatures.

It Is The Divinity Flowing Into Us And Out To All, And Back To God;

And His Divine Will Does Not Return Void But With Our Return Of Love For Us And For All.

This Is A New and Higher Divine Life That Is Now Available On Earth.

As We Continuously Call Jesus Into Doing Our Acts, We Are Raised From A Human To A Divine Life.

If Jesus Does Our Acts- In Us, These Are Divine Acts.

We Don't Become Divine Persons, We Always Remain Human Creatures, But We Are Raised Up

To A Divine Life With God– By Participation In His Intimate Interior Life At His Own Divine Level.

The Gift Of The Divine Will Is The Gift That Everyone Can Individually Live In; But Those Living In It – All Share In God Together.

And This Living In The Divine Will Blesses God And Everyone To The Degree That That Are Interiorly Disposed To Receive It.

This Gift Is No Small Matter.

God Uses this Gift To Bring About The Era Of Peace For The Whole World.

God Has Prepared This Gift As Refuge and Preparation For Us To Live a New And Higher Existence As Human Beings.

Living In This Gift, We Are Sanctified And Prepared To Live In The Era Of Peace.

We Are Re-created To Live As Adam and Eve Did Before The Fall.

Jesus Told Luisa That He Has A Whole New Generation Of Humans Inside Him.

We Are Being Re-created In The Divine Will

To Live In The Era Of Peace.

"The Greatest Gift"

The Sun Of My Will

The Sun Of My Will

Biography of] Luisa Piccarreta By Maria Rosaria Del Genio Published By The Vatican, Copyright 2015– Dicastero per la Communicazione– Libreria Editrice Vaticana

P. 220,

"Here Is What Clearly Appears:

This "Living in the Divine Will of Jesus" is the Greatest Gift" that He wants to give people. It is an "overflow" of His Mercy, because It is His Nature to want "to splurge even more in pouring out His love."

Love beckons love. Realizing that Jesus has given them everything and that He has no other

Gift greater than the Possession of His Will to give in order to be Loved, people will be able to cherish "the Great Good they possess" and love Him with it.

Clearly this reciprocity looks very much like the Heavenly Love between the Divine Persons in the Most Holy Trinity!

In other words, Luisa Piccarreta tells us that remaining in The Divine Will means adhering to it completely without leaving any gaps.

[It Is Continuous] It is like when someone wants to glue two pieces of glass together, they must not be any air bubbles that will keep them from bonding perfectly.

This is how people if they want can adhere to God without leaving any "air bubbles" between them.

How is this possible? How can the great glass pane that is god be united to the smaller piece of glass that is the human person?"

FORGET SELF

One Of The Best Advice For Living In The Divine Will I Have Ever Heard:

"It Is Important To Remember that having desired the Gift- and after deciding to sacrifice one's own will, that it is only Jesus who does all the work."

Divine Will Booklet With Ecclesiastical Approval TRANI, Italy, October 17, 1997, Carmelo Casati Archbishop of Trani Barletta-Bisceglie.

Golden Rule

"GOLDEN RULE: WE DESIRE IT AND JESUS DOES ALL THE WORK."

HOW TO RECEIVE THE GIFT OF THE DIVINE WILL.

"To receive the Gift of the Divine Will one needs the desire to receive it, and to decide to no longer

give life to one's own human will. Jesus said: "…
you don't need paths, nor doors, nor keys to enter
into My Divine Will… To enter creatures need but
remove the Pebble of their own will…
 A soul has but to desire it and all is done, My Will
assumes all the work…"

Book Of Heaven – Feb 16, 1921

"It Is Important To Remember that having
desired the Gift after deciding to sacrifice one's
own will, that it is only Jesus who does all the
work." "Only Jesus can do a Divine Act. We always
remain as creatures, surrendering to His Most
Holy Will."

A LESSON FOR LIFE: FORGET SELF

"From the first moment a soul decides to
embrace living in the Divine Will, they must learn
to forget themselves. Jesus says that there is only
one way of achieving this, and *that* it must be
practiced for the rest of your life:

"My daughter, in order for the soul to be able to forget herself – everything she does or has to do must be done as if I wanted to do it in her.

If she prays, she should say: 'It is Jesus who wants to pray, and I pray together with Him.' If she works: 'it is Jesus who wants to work, it is Jesus who wants to walk, it is Jesus who wants to eat, who wants to sleep, who wants to get up, who wants to enjoy Himself.' And it should be like that in everything for the rest of her life, excluding errors.

Only in this manner is the soul able to forget herself.

For not only will she do everything because I want it, but because I want to do it, she will need me."

Book Of Heaven – August 14, 1912

"Everything should be now done with reference to Jesus because it is He who is doing everything within us– except error, i.e.. sin."

"WHAT IF I SIN?

If we sin, we would lose the Gift of DW.

This is because we obviously cannot make Jesus sin. If we make a sincere act of contrition then we can ask Jesus to return the Gift to us, and He will do so."

The Pearl Of Great Price

The Divine Will Is The Pearl Of Great Price That We Have Found, And We Forget Everything Else And Buy The Field.

This Gift Is A Paradigm Shift!

A Fundamental Change In Approach And Underlying Circumstances.

(Oxford Dictionaries)

Forget About Self, And Let God Take Over-

This Is The Nugget To Remember To Shift Our Life Into Living With One Will

Alone- God's Will. This Is What Our Spiritual Life Is All About-
And That Only Happens Completely In the Gift Of Living In The Divine Will.

That Is What Happens In Purgatory, And This Is Purgatory Now Ahead Of Time - In The Gift Of The Divine Will On Earth.

After We Turn Over Our Human Will To God's Will — We Forget About Ourselves And Let God Take Over.

But This Living In The Divine Will Is No Quietism - We Forget About Ourselves As Jesus Takes Over Control Of Our Lives-

But We Are Attentive And Call Jesus Into Doing
All Our Acts And Accompany Him In Everything
He Does In Us Now And In Heaven For Eternity.

In The Midst Of The Darkness!

Even Now On Earth, When Are All Wrapped Up In Their Own Human Will, We Have A New Will To Run Our Life!

God Is Offering Us Heaven And More!

A New Divine Life That Is Our Birthright And Our Heritage That We Never Could Have Imagined Or Dreamed That He Would Give Us.

He Is Giving Us His Own Beating Heart!

To take over Operative Life Of our life!

God's Heart Is Called The Divine Will – And It's Ours,

If Only, WE WILL STILL BELIEVE THAT GOD IS GOOD,

AND GOD IS ABLE,

AND THAT WE CAN BE THE GENERATION THAT RECEIVES JESUS BACK–

And Listen To Him Speaking To Us Today. BECAUSE THIS IS WHAT IS HAPPENING On Earth

How Can A Person Possess A Divine Will?

How Can A Person Possess A Divine Will?

That's The Way We Were Designed To Live From The Beginning

We Humans Have A Human Will That Runs Our Life. And That Is Good, And That Is The Way We Were Designed And Created To Be; And That Will Always Be.

But Humans Were Designed And Created To Have Our Human Will To Be Possessed And Overseen And Operated By God's Divine Will.

What HAPPENED?

The Original Sin Changed The State Of Our Human Nature.

How Could Adam And Eve Be Disobedient?

Jesus Tells Luisa That They Forgot That God Loved Them.

They Took The Garden Of Eden For Granted.

Adam And Eve Pulled Their Human Will Out Of The Divine Will

And Decided To Run Their Own Lives By Their Human Will Alone–

Outside Of God's Divine Will.

God Withdrew His Divine Will From The Human Will; and that is the "Fallen" Human Nature That We Received.

We are Missing The Divine Will That We Need To Live A Whole And Integrated Life.

Now, In Our Time, God Has Given The Divine Will Back To Luisa Piccarreta For Her and For All Humans.

We Just Have To Learn About This Gift Of Living In The Divine Will, Sign Ourselves Over To It, And Live In It.

Creation and The Redemption Are Ongoing.

Creation and The Redemption Are Not Finished Until The Sanctification Is Finished

The Gift Is The Capstone And The Fulfillment Of The New Covenant – ...And Now We Know "The Rest Of The Redemption Story."

We Knew About The Redemption, How Jesus Saves Us, But Not How The Sanctification would take place, even Though The Bible Clearly States That It's Coming.

The Last Supper

Jesus At The Last Supper Discourse Tells Us That The Holy Spirit Will Reveal More Of Himself.

Jesus Tells Luisa That When He Reveals Himself, It Is To Make A Gift Of Himself.

He Is Pouring Himself Out Completely In This Gift And It Is Available To Everyone.

This Gift is The Sanctification Of Humanity; and Jesus told Luisa that He always meant The Sanctification to be simple and easy to do.

- And it is, to the degree that we are willing to give ourselves completely to God - as He gives Himself completely to us. We Must Sign Over Our Human Will And Let God Completely Run Out Lives.

This Is Not That Difficult Folks!

We Must be willing to learn about this Gift, and to make the Greatest Of Sacrifices:

We Use Our Free Will To Call Down The Divine Will And Sign Ourselves Over To It Running Our Lives For Eternity.

The Easiest Way To Explain This Gift – And How It's Accomplished In Us: Is That It's A Divine Possession.

Jesus went out of his way to make sure that we knew what an evil possession was.

When Jesus was on earth 2,000 years ago, He pointed it out how a demonic possession worked, and what's involved in that.

And so we know how a person gives the consent of their human will, and signs themselves over to the demon.

With our human will, we can make a contract with the devil.

But God wants us to make use of our same human will to sign ourselves over to Him and His Divine Will.

And so, instead of living with our human will running our life, we turn ourselves over to God's Divine Will Running Our Life.

The Divine Will enters Into us and possesses us, and He takes over us completely, and runs our life. We must be willing to have God Direct Our Life in all things as we accompany Him.

We Must Desire that He Controls Us Completely.

We desire Him to take over driving the spiritual vehicle of our body and soul; and we are happy to just sit on his lap and accompany Him while **God Drives Our Life.**

God Offers Us This New Covenant That He Gave Us – The Gift of The Divine Will – We Just Have To Willingly And Completely Agree To His Terms.

We Have To Sign Onto This Divine Will Covenant. We Give Him Our Human Will Completely And He Takes Over Our Life With His Divine Will Completely.

It's An Exchange Of Wills– His Will Completely takes Over And Operates Our Human Will. This Is Offered To Everyone– Everyone Alive Right Now On Earth, who will learn about it, desire it, and sign ourselves Over To It, And Live In It.

The Central Message

The Central Message Of Jesus To Luisa is Love and Mercy-

We Are All Given The Same Divine Will To Fix Our Problems And Give Us A New Start For Humanity-

To Live A New and Higher Divine Life And Give A Return Of Love to The Father At the Divine Level That He Deserves.

The Central Problem With The Human Condition Is That We Are Living In A Defective Fallen Nature and God Has Given Us The Cure– The Fix. It Is Called The Gift Of The Divine Will.

(All We Have To Do Is Learn About It, Receive It, And Live In It.)

First Of All, You Must Know How Human Beings Operate:

A Human Being Has A Soul Which Animates And Gives Life To Our Body.

The Human Soul

The Human Soul Has Three Main Parts, Also Called Faculties, Or Powers.

They Are The Will, The Intellect, And The Memory.

Our Human Will Is Our Primary Faculty Of Our Soul.

The Human Will Along With Our Intellect And Memory Runs Our Soul And Our Human Life.

This Is How God Created Us And Is The Central Aspect Of Our Being And Will Always Be Such.

Our Human Will Is The Greatest And Most Beautiful Part Of Our Being- When It Is Connected To God.

Human Beings Were Designed And Created To Have Our Human Will- Connected To And Run By God's Divine Will.

But Adam And Eve, Our First Parents Pulled Their Human Will Out Of The Divine Will – Which Was In Complete Control Of Their Human Will And Their Lives– And Decided To Run Their Lives On Their Own With Just Their Human Will.

The Human Will Was Never Meant To Control And Operate Our Human Life On Its Own.

Here Is The Crux Of The Matter:

The words of Our Lady– **In The Book: The Virgin Mary In The Kingdom Of the Divine Will by Luisa Piccarreta:**

"The creature, with its human will, is all vacillating, weak, inconstant, disordered."

And this is so because God in creating it, created it united as in nature with His Divine Will in such a way that it should be the strength, the prime movement, the support, the food, the life of the human will.

Thus, by not giving life of the Divine Will in ours, the goods received from God in the Creation are rejected and also the rights received in nature in the act in which we were created."

THE TRINITY

The Divine Will Is

The Central Mystery Of The Trinity.

God's Divine Will That We Are Talking About Is The Actual Source And Operative Life Of The Trinity. All Three Persons Of The Trinity Hold The Divine Will In Common.

From the pamphlet, The Kingdom of the Divine Will, Copyright 1995, The Luisa Piccarreta Center of the Divine Will Jacksonville, FL 32210:

"Fiat!

"Dearly beloved of God we would like to introduce you to a very beautiful story about God in his Divine Will and how the Divine Will wishes to reign on earth as it does in Heaven; For the time has now arrived.

Part I

In the beginning, before all Creation came into being, was God. God is a Trinity of Persons: Father, Son, and Holy Spirit.

Their Persons are distinct; yet they are Perfect.

They are a perfect unity of oneness in Being, Essence, and Will.

The highest and most beautiful thing that can be said of Them is that they have but one Will among themselves; Thus, there is the most perfect unity, harmony, peace and delight.

With the infinite power of this Divine Will, The Three Divine Persons continually produce new and increasing joys and happiness and delights among Themselves.

Their Kingdom is Their Divine Will, the same Kingdom that we pray to come on earth when we recite the Lord's Prayer."

God Is Giving Us The Cure For All Our Problems

This Same Divine Will Which Runs The Trinity Is Designed In Our Creation To Have Operational Control Of Our Human Lives And Run Our Souls And Our Lives.

Thus We Would Have The Harmony That The Trinity Has Within It And Be Part Of Its Intimate Inner Life. Adam And Eve Lost The Divine Will And We Have Been Given It Back.

The Human Will Acting On Its Own Is The Central Problem In Human Existence– The Only One That Exists.

This Is The Most Important Message For Humanity At This Time:

God Is Offering Us:

To Sign Ourselves Over To His Divine Will Possessing Us Completely

It Is One Thing To Know That We Are Habitations For God– But God Is Offering Us To Sign Ourselves Over To God Possessing Us Completely, The Way We Were Meant To Be Originally Before The Fall.

We Turn Over Our Human Will To Him– And He Connects Up And Fuses His Divine Will Into Us

– And Enters In And Pours The Same Source And Operative Life From The Center Of The Trinity Into Our Human Will And In This Way God Possesses Our Human Will, Our Mind And Our Memory–

The Three Faculties/Powers/ Parts Of Our Soul And Takes Complete Control Of All Our Acts– Our Actions Interiorly And Exteriorly.

This Is How God Lives In Us- In Our Soul And Actions.

This Is How Humans Are Happy And The Way We Were Supposed To Live From The Beginning.

This is Our Birthright And Our Heritage.

This Is How God Is Reclaiming Humanity And The Earth.

We Call Jesus Into Doing All Our Acts

We Call Jesus Into Doing All Our Acts And He Enters In With The Divine Will which Contains The Trinity And All Of God.

We Still And Always Have Free Will– Because Our Free Will Wants This Divine Possession Of the Divine Will Of God – Which Contains All Of God– And Thus We Contain All Of God.

It's God Giving Himself Completely To Us And We Give Ourselves Completely To God.

We Become One With Jesus, As Jesus Is One With The Father, And The Holy Spirit.

They All Have The Same Heart– The Same Will, – And In The Divine Will So Do We.

This Is How A Human Being Is Connected To And Contains God. Hell Is Populated With People That Said No To The Gift Of Living In The Divine Will.

This Is No Small Thing That God Is Offering Us This Gift Now On Earth.

This is The Time Of Decision.

Living Hosts

We Are Created To Be Habitations Of God.

We Become Living Hosts In The Living In The Divine Will; We Call Jesus Into Doing All Our Actions In Us, To Carry Out All Our Activities.

If Jesus Is Doing Our Acts, They Become Divine Acts. We Don't Become Divine Persons; We Always Remain Human Persons, But We Are Raised Up To Live A Divine Life By Participation In The Divine Life Of God.

In The Divine Will, God Possesses Our Human Will And Thus Lives In Our Acts- Which Are Raised From A Human Act To A Divine Act.

In The Eucharist, God Lives In The "substance" Of the bread and wine- while we still perceive the 'accidents' of Bread And Wine. The 'accidents" are the qualities that the human perceives- it looks and tastes like bread and wine- even though it is now The Body, Blood, Soul, and Divinity of Jesus.

Jesus told Luisa that the only reason that He could Transubstantiate the bread and wine into Himself, is because there is no will that opposes His Will.

"Christs body remains in the communicant as long as the accidents remain themselves." (www.ewtn.com- EWTN, Transubstantiation)

Jesus told Luisa That He Only stays about 15 minutes until The Eucharist is dissolved. God Does Not Live In Us Bodily As He Lives In The Accidents Of The Eucharist- The Mode Of God Is

To Possess Our Human Will And To Live In Our Acts.

The Human Will Must Have No Will Which Opposes Gods Will. In The Gift Of Living In The Divine Will - The Human Will Is Fused With The Divine Will Which Takes Over The Human Will. Because God Gave Us Free Will - We Must Sign Over Our Human Will To Allow God's Will To Take Over Our Human Will. God Flows And Possesses Us With And In His Divine Will Which contains All Of Him. (I am not a theologian, and this is my understanding.)

The Sanctity Of Sanctities

Book Of Heaven –March 15, 1912

The Divine Will Is The Sanctity Of Sanctities. The souls who live in the Divine Will are true living hosts.

Words Of Luisa:

"Continuing in my usual state, I felt a great desire to do the Most Holy Will of blessed Jesus; And He, on coming, told me: "My daughter, my Will is the Sanctity of Sanctities.

The soul who does my Will, however small, ignorant, unknown, leaves the other Saints behind in spite of their prodigies, sensational conversions and miracles.

Rather, in comparison, the souls who do my Will are queens, and it is as if all the others were at their service. It seems that the souls who do my Will do nothing, while they do everything, because, being in my Will, they act in a Divine Manner, in a hidden and surprising way.

So, they are light that illuminates, they are winds that purify, they are fire that burns, they are miracles that make others do miracles.

Those who do miracles are channels; but in these souls resides the power.

Therefore, they are the foot of the missionary, the tongue of the preachers, the strength of the week, the patience of the sick, the regime of the superiors, the obedience of the subjects, the tolerance of the slandered, the firmness in dangers, the heroism of the heroes, the courage of the martyrs, the sanctity in the Saints, and so with all the rest.

Being in My Will, they concur with all the good that can exist both in Heaven and on earth.

This is why I can truly say that they are My True Hosts – but Living Hosts, not dead ones.

In fact the accidents [the bread and wine in Holy Communion] that form the host are not full of life, nor do they influence my life; but the soul is full of life, and by doing my Will, she influences and concurs with all that I do.

<u>This is why these Hosts consecrated by My Will are more dear to me than the very Sacramental</u>

<u>*Hosts, and if I have reason to exist in the Sacramental Hosts, it is to form the Sacramental Hosts of My Will."*</u>

"My daughter, I take such delight in My Will, that in simply hearing one speak about It, I feel overjoyed and I call the whole of Heaven to make feast.

Imagine, yourself, what will become of those souls who do It: in them I find all the contentment's, and to them I give all the continents; *Their Life is The Life Of The Blessed.*

Two things only do they cherish, desire and yearn: my Will and Love. They have little to do, while indeed they do everything.

The virtues themselves remain absorbed in my Will and in Love, and so they have nothing to do with them anymore, since my Will contains, possesses and absorbs everything – but in a way which is Divine, Immense and Endless.

This is the life of the Blessed."

The Pearl Of Great Price

Our Job Is To Live In The Divine Will And To Do Our Acts In The Divine Will.

Excerpt From The Book: *Be Faithful And Attentive* By Robert T. Hart , Copyright 2005, Luisa Piccarreta Center For The Divine Will Caryville, TN A Handbook For Living In The Divine Will, pp.26-27

"What does God expect of a soul to whom He has chosen to give his Adorable Will?

He expects this soul to BE FAITHFUL AND ATTENTIVE at working to never do her own will, but only God's, and, of learning to continually call His Divine Will into all her acts.

In this way, little by little, the soul will come to fully possess God, and God to fully possess the soul. The soul also has also been given the great responsibility (and privilege!) of bringing God's

Kingdom to earth, transforming the earth into a terrestrial paradise.”

Book Of Heaven – Volume 19 – September 13, 1926

Jesus told Luisa:

“to reestablish the Kingdom of my Will on earth, there must be sufficient acts by creatures to keep my Kingdom from remaining suspended and enable it to descend and take form upon the very acts which creatures have formed in order to obtain such an immense good.

That is why I urge you so much to make your rounds in all our works, our Creation and Redemption.

I do it to have you contribute your acts, your ‘I love You,’ your adoration, your recognition and your ‘I thank you,’ over all our works... Then, if, in truth, you want this Kingdom, continue your act so that when the established number has been completed, you can obtain that for which you sighed with so much insistence.

…"Do you see, then, dear soul, what great work God wants to accomplish by your acts, done in his Will? Realize deeply both the immense privilege and responsibility Almighty God has given you!

What an ungrateful wretch you indeed would be if you did not consider the Gift of the Divine Will To be the "pearl of great price" mentioned in the Gospel, at which finding you might "sell all" and purchase the pearl.

This "selling all" is none other than giving up your own will – and doing so constantly – to allow the Divine Will to operate in you.

When you have learned to never do your own will, but only to operate with his, continuously in all the ups and downs of life and all the trials and sorrows God will send you, and when you come to that point that you would rather die than do a single act of your own will, you will have "sold all" and the "pearl of great price" - God's Divine Will- will be your own possession!"

"To encourage you on this long journey, keep in mind that even just one act in the Divine Will is a Divine Act and worth more than Heaven and earth.

Just one act done in the Divine Will gives more glory to God than all the acts of all the previous Saints and martyrs combined.

Remember too that God does not expect you to be successful in remaining always in his Divine Will all at once since you are in the habit of always living in your own will.

He does however as mentioned above expected diligent effort to make constant use of this Gift."

One Instant In The Divine Will

The Soul That Does Her Acts In The Divine Will On Earth

Book Of Heaven – March 8, 1914"

"My daughter those who live in my will can claim all that I do as their very own.

And this is because the soul's will, having given itself to me, remains so identified with Me that it does everything that my Will does–

"... Whereby, dying to this life the soul in My Will carries within itself all the celebrated Masses, all the prayers and all the good works that are performed, since they are all fruits of my Will."

"However they are much less in comparison with the action of my Will Itself, which the soul carries within itself as its own.

"One instant of this action of my Will is enough to surpass all the actions of all creatures, past, present and future." "

For that reason, the soul that dies in my Will acquires a beauty beyond all beauty.

And nothing else can compare with it neither height nor riches, nor sanctity, nor wisdom, nor love. Nothing, nothing can compare with it, nothing can match it. *That's the soul that dies fused in my will, upon making its entry into its Heavenly Homeland, will find not only the doors of Heaven opening up to it but all of Heaven lowering Itself to allow the soul to enter its celestial dwelling and to honor the action of my Will in it.*

What then can I tell you concerning the feast and surprise of all the Blessed upon seeing this soul, entirely sealed with the work of the Divine Will. What can be said of this soul that has done everything in my Will, having done every word, thought, and work in my Will?

These will be so many suns that will adorn it, each different from the other in light and beauty. And upon seeing in this soul so many divine rivers, the Blessed will be inundated. Heaven, not being able to contain these Divine rivers, they will flow upon the earth for the good of souls.''

"Ah, my daughter! My Will is the portent of portents; It is the secret for finding light, holiness, riches.

It is the secret of all goods.

But if It is not intimately known, It cannot consequently be appreciated nor loved as It merits.

Appreciate It, then, and love It, and make I known to whoever you see that is disposed.''

"Another day, while I was suffering, I felt as if I could not do anything; And I felt oppressed by this. And Jesus embracing my whole being, said to me: "My daughter, don't be troubled.

Seek only to remain abandoned in my Will and I will do everything for you.

For only one instant in my Will is worth more than all the good that you could do in your entire lifetime."

"I also remember that on another day he told me:

"My daughter, he who truly does my Will can say that everything that takes place within him - be it in his soul or body – whatever he feels, whatever he suffers, takes place in Me.

Thus he can say: 'Jesus suffers, Jesus is oppressed.' For everything that creatures do to me reaches the soul who does my Will, for I dwell in that soul."...

"...On another day He said to me: "My daughter, the soul who does my Will never enter Purgatory because my Will purges the soul of everything."

"And having held on to it so jealously in life, guarding it in my Will, how could I possibly permit the fires of Purgatory to touch it?

And at the most, should it happen to be lacking in some adornment, then my Will, before revealing the Divinity to it, will go about clothing it with all the garments it needs; and then I will reveal Myself."

Divine Acts

A Prime Idea In The Divine Will:

Everything We Do Outside The Divine Will Is Finite And Limited- Done With Our Selfish Human Will - – All Our Acts Done In The Human Will Alone - Outside Of The Divine Will- Are As Filthy Rags- Are Nauseous And Hold No Enchantment For God

Everything We Do In The Divine Will – Our Acts Are Divine Acts And Light!

All Of Heaven Looks Down To See Who Is Doing These Acts. We Call Jesus Into Doing All Our Acts – And If Jesus Is Doing Our Acts, They Become Divine Acts- Meaning "of God"- God's Acts- Done In And Through Us –These Are Divine Lives Of Jesus That Will Live Forever-They Are Eternal – That Is Why We Venerate Jesus On the Cross-

Did You Know That Every Act That Jesus Did On Earth – And In Heaven Will Live Forever?

Sanctification

All The Earth Has Been Awaiting The Sanctification

Book Of Heaven –

Volume 17– September 17, 1924

"... Do you see what it means to do acts in my Will?

This is to live in my Will: the Sun of my Will, transforming the human will into Sun, acts in it as if in Its own center."

Ephesians 2:1–5 KJV "

"And you hath he quickened, who were dead in trespasses and sins; Wherein in time past ye walked according to the course of this world, according to the prince of the power of the air, the spirit that now worketh in the children of disobedience:

Among whom also we had our conversation in times past in the lusts of our flesh, fulfilling the desires of the flesh and of the mind; and were by nature the children of wrath, even as others.

But God, who is rich in mercy, for his great love wherewith he loved us, Even when we were dead in sins, hath quickened us together with Christ, (by grace ye are saved;)

We Are Cleansed

"But we are all as an unclean thing, and all our righteousness are as filthy rags; and we all do fade as a leaf; and our Iniquities, like the wind, have taken us away."

Isaiah 64:6 – KJV

"But they that wait upon the LORD shall renew their strength; they shall mount up with wings as eagles; they shall run, and not be weary; and they shall walk, and not faint."

Isaiah 40:31 - KJV

"But as it is written, Eye hath not seen, nor ear heard, neither have entered into the heart of man, the things which God hath prepared for them that love him."

1 Corinthians 2:9 KJV

"Behold ye among the heathen, and regard, and wonder marvelously: for I will work a wonder in your days, which ye will not believe though it be told to you."

Habakkuk 1:5 - KJV

God Takes Control Of Our Life

God Gave Us Free Will And That Free Will Is Never Taken Away.

We Use Our Free Will To Learn about the Divine Will– Sign Ourselves Over To It, and To Continually Offer It Up To The Father.

This Is The Living In The Divine Will That Adam and Eve Possessed.

In Everything We Do We Call Jesus Into Doing All Our Acts In Us.

Yes, We Sign Over All Our Rights To God, But We Retain Our Human Freedom Which We Lock Into God's Will; Continually Offering It Up To The Father.

The Final Signature

At First, We Take The Divine Will On Loan,

But When God Sees that We Are Ready,

He Confirms This Gift To Us On Earth And For Eternity.

Volume 18 – December 25, 1925

"... to live in my Will is a Gift and the possession of the greatest Gift. But this Gift that contains infinite value

... is not given except to one who is disposed and should not waste it.

And to one who will esteem and love it so much, even more than its own life, that it is ready to sacrifice its own life in order to let this Gift of my Volition have supremacy over all, esteeming it more than life itself.

Indeed, one's own life is nothing in comparison to it.

Therefore, first I want to see that the soul truly wants to do my Will and never its own, that it is ready to sacrifice anything to do Mine, and that in all it does, it asked Me always, even on loan, the Gift of my Volition.

When I see that it does everything with the loan of my Volition, I give it to the soul as a Gift, because by asking for it again and again, it has formed the empty space in its soul in which to put the Celestial Gift.

Living habitually on the loan of this Divine Food, it has lost the taste for its own volition; Its palate is ennobled and is not adapted to the vile foods of its own ego.

Therefore seeing itself in possession of the Gift that it longed for, yearned for, and loved so much, the soul will live by the Life of that Gift, will love It and will give It the esteem that it merits.

… here is why there is so much necessity of dispositions, of knowledge of the Gift, and of the esteem and appreciation, and of loving the Gift itself.

Therefore, the forerunner of the Gift that I want to give to the creature of my Will is the Knowledge of It.

The Knowledge

The Knowledge prepares the way.

Knowledge is as the contract that I want to make for the Gift which I wish to give.

For however much knowledge enters into the soul so much more is it stimulated to desire the Gift and to *solicit the* **Divine Writer** *to* **sign** **his** **final** **signature so that the Gift is its own and the soul possesses it.**

 So in these times, the sign that I want to give this Gift of my Volition is the Knowledge of it.

Therefore, be attentive and do not flee from anything that I have manifested to you about my Will, if you want me to place my last signature on the Gift that I long to give to creatures"

The Three Appeals

Three Appeals Document – Luisa Piccarreta

book of heaven.com–
(The following are words with Jesus gives to his children through Luisa Piccarreta, 1925)

Divine Appeal

"With His Father and The Holy Spirit, The Divine King appeals to his children on earth to come now and enter into The Kingdom of His Will."

… "My dear and beloved children I have prepared everything for you in My Humanity and I have prayed for and obtained graces, helps, light and strength for you to receive a Gift so great.

On my part I have done everything; so now I am waiting for you to do your part.

Who would be so ungrateful as to turn me away and not welcome the gift that I'm bringing to you?

Know that my love is so much and I will forget all about your past life, your sins, all your evils;

and I will bury them all in the ocean of my love to burn them all away;

And then we will begin a new life together, all of my will.

How To Enter In

How To Enter Into Living In The Gift Of The Divine Will.

HE WILL FORGET ALL ABOUT OUR PAST LIFE, OUR SINS, ALL OUR EVILS- AND CAST THEM ALL AWAY- AND WE WILL BEGIN A NEW LIFE TOGETHER — HIS WILL IS TAKING OVER OUR MISERABLE LIFE- NOW- AS WE SAY YES TO HIS GIFT!

DEAR READER,

YOU KNOW ENOUGH TO SAY YES -AND LET GOD TAKE OVER YOUR LIFE.
IT HAPPENS INSTANTANEOUSLY!

We Just Have To Stay In It Continuously.

We give our Fiat in union with The Blessed Virgin's Fiat when She said Yes at the Annunciation. Jesus was conceived in Her instantaneously and that is what happens in us when we say Yes to This Gift.

At First, We Take This Gift On Loan.

We still have to learn about it we still have to receive it every day as God transforms us and transubstantiate us into a New Divine Life and eventually, we will be confirmed in The Divine Will for eternity.

We don't become Divine Persons, we always remain human creatures, but we call Jesus to come into us and to do all our acts; and if Jesus is doing our acts, our acts become Divine Acts and we are raised from a human to a Divine Life by participation in the Divine Life of God!

So call Jesus into doing all your acts- over and over - and sign yourself over to this Divine Life. It Is God Giving Himself Completely to Us and We Are Giving Ourselves Completely To Him!

It's a Divine Possession. PEOPLE, WE NEED THIS NEW HIGHER LIFE – THIS IS NO SMALL

THING – WE ARE COMING INTO A DESTRUCTION OF MOST OF THIS GENERATION AND MOST OF THE EARTH! This Can Be Lessened By Prayer And Sacrifice.

But most importantly our human will operating in a fallen nature, is failing us, and we need God's new energy and power- and for Him to take over complete control of our lives.

This New And Higher Way Of Living Is Our Refuge!

WHAT IF NOAH AND HIS FAMILY DIDN'T GET INTO THE ARK?

WE NEED THIS GIFT OF LIVING IN GODS WILL- TO MAKE IT THROUGH ANY DESTRUCTION THAT HAS ALREADY BEGUN!

Time is short people.

This Gift Of Living In The Divine Will Is Our Refuge, But You Still Have To Learn About It, Sign Yourself Over To It, And Live In It!

You And I Need This Gift!

It Is The Gift Of God Himself Coming Down From Heaven And Into Our Souls!

Look around you! The World is Being Flooded With Evil - And This Gift Of The Divine Will Is Our Safe Refuge To Keep Our Sanity and To Become Transformed In Holiness.

All Is Coming Together In this Gift!

In The Spiritual Life Your Heart Is Your Will–

What You Want – There Is Your Treasure– Where Your Heart Is.

This Gift Is The Refuge Of The Immaculate Heart Of Mary And The Sacred Heart Of Jesus.

Their Hearts Are The Same Divine Will!

We Are Lifted Up In The Spiritual Ark Of The Covenant- Our Lady – And Set Down in The Era Of Peace- The Rest Of The Seventh Day.

In This Gift We Are Being Not Just Regenerated But Recreated In the Image And Likeness Of God – The Way Humans Were Created From The Beginning – Before The Fall. You Do Not Want To Miss This Ark Of Refuge. Get In The Boat Now!!!

Jesus further exhorts us in this same Fatherly Appeal:

[This Is Jesus Speaking!]

"Who would have the heart to refuse me and send me away without accepting my visit which is so full of a father's love?

But, if you will welcome me, I will remain with you as a Father in the midst of his children. Then we must be in the greatest accord and live together with one will alone.

Oh! how much I long for this; how I moan, how I cry, even going into delirium, and weeping because I want my dearest children to gather around Me and live with My very Own Will.

... And since you do not come back to me, I come in search of you because I can no longer contain the love that consumes me; And I am bringing you the great Gift of My Will...

Oh I beg you, I plead with you, be moved to compassion for my so many tears and sighs!! I come to you not only as a Father but also as a Teacher among his disciples... I want you to listen to Me because I will be teaching you surprising things, lessons of Heaven, which will carry with them a Light that will never go out and a blazing Love which endures forever.

My lessons will give you a divine strength, an invisible invincible courage, a holiness which keeps growing more and more.

These lessons will light the way for your steps and will guide along the way to your Heavenly Fatherland. ... I come as a King to live among His people, But not for the purpose of levying taxes and heaping burdens upon you. No. No.

I come because I want your will, your miseries, your weaknesses, all your evils. My sovereignty is really this; I want everything that distresses you and causes you to be unhappy and restless so that I can hide it within my love and burn it all away.

As beneficent, pacific, and magnanimous King that I am, I want to exchange My Will for yours, filling you with my most tender Love, with my Riches and Happiness, with my Peace and my most pure Joy.

If you will give Me your will all will be done just as I have said; And you will make Me happy, and you will be happy too.

I long for nothing else than for My Will to reign among you.

(Words which Jesus gives to his children through Luisa Piccarreta, 1925)" ...

[This Is Jesus HIMSELF SPEAKING THROUGH LUISA!!! YOU CAN SIMPLY DO A SEARCH OF BOOK OF HEAVEN AND READ 36 VOLUMES OF JESUS' OWN WORDS TO LUISA!!!

His Sheep Will Recognize His Voice!

"My sheep hear my voice, and I know them, and they follow Me."
John 10:27–28 KJV

This Gift Has Never Been Available To Fallen Creatures that We Are!

THIS IS NOT THAT DIFFICULT PEOPLE! IT IS NOT A CHANGE IN YOUR CIRCUMSTANCES – AT LEAST NOT AT FIRST- IT'S A CHANGE IN WHAT WILL IS RUNNING YOUR LIFE-

GOD WANTS TO EXCHANGE OUR LOW, LIMITED, MISERABLE WILL FOR HIS DIVINE WILL – COMING DOWN FROM THE CENTER OF THE TRINITY- WHICH ACTUALLY TAKES OVER COMPLETE CONTROL AND DIRECTS OUR Human Will And Our LIFE AND ACTUALLY DOES ALL OUR ACTS!

This Is What Our Spiritual Life Is All About- After We Turn Over Our Human Will To God's Will – We Forget About Ourselves And Let God's Will Take Over Control Of Our Life! We Give Him All Rights

Over Our Life And He Takes Over Total Control. He Drives The Vehicle Of Our Life and Soul. And He Lets Us Sit On His Lap. We Simply Accommodate And Accompany Him In All The Actions And Circumstances Of Our Life. Oh! What A Relief And A Joy!

Forgiveness

Will Jesus Forgive Me?

The Way Of Divine Love
Jesus to Sister Josefa Menendez:

"Oh! All of you who are steeped in sin, and who for a time more or less long have lived as wanderers and fugitives because of your crimes.

Do not yield to despair! For as long as a breath of life remains, a man may have recourse to mercy and ask for pardon."

Mary's Heart

Mary's Maternal Heart Is One With The Divine Will.

The Sacred Heart Of Jesus, And The Immaculate Heart Of Mary Are One Heart- The Divine Will.

And God Wants Us To Share This Same Divine Will - The Heart Of God With Us

Sun Of My Will- Page 227:

"Dying on the cross, Jesus wanted His Mother to become the Mother of all people, and He wanted that She do for all creatures what She did for Him. This was one of the greatest graces that He gave humanity.

Therefore Her Maternity extends to all the acts of all people, so that Jesus may see them all protected and tucked away in Her maternal love.

So, just as His inseparable Mama extended Her Maternity inside and outside of Jesus' Humanity, God established Her and confirmed Her as Mother of every creature's thought, breath, heartbeat and word. In the end Jesus will share His place in Mary's Maternal Heart with whoever decides to live in His Divine Will.

[Mary's Maternal Heart Is The Divine Will. And She Gives Us Lessons On How To Enter Into This Divine Eden]

Book: The Sun Of My Will
[Biography of] Luisa Piccarreta By Maria

Rosaria Del Genio Published By The Vatican, Copyright 2015– Dicastero per la Communicazione– Libreria Editrice Vaticana P.227

Luisa Piccarreta's Mission

"Being bedridden does not isolate Luisa. She is ready to see reality as God sees it. She can love people as God loves them. She can feel compassion as God feels it; she can touch everything like God touches it with a purity of heart and humility. And physically she can even bring food back up transformed in "the aroma of Christ. (cf. 2 Cor 2:15)

Luisa follows her path of suffering and Love, which is welcomed and offered. And as a lay woman, she is doing her part in the church *by unleashing that spiritual energy that offers a fruitful service to others.* People see her in bed and, even if they are not always consciously aware of it, they intuit that her bedridden state reveals something else. It is though it were a physically tangible representation of something deeper that cannot be seen. It is only by knowing what goes on in her heart that it is, in fact, possible to know that being confined to bed is both the how and the why of her being rooted in the heart of the Divine Will!

If that phenomenon of physical rigidity has not happened to her, who would have ever noticed her? Nevertheless, that which appears extraordinary about her life and the eyes of many serves Jesus for making Luisa live in the ordinary, and for realizing in her, an image of the creature envisioned by God in his original plan. What is extraordinary about Luisa, therefore, refers back to the ordinary, better yet, to normality. Once again, Luisa's life invites us to see things upside down"

Answered Prayer

Jesus Has Appeared And Has Answered Our Prayers

The Problem Is With The Condition Of Human Beings. We Are Out Of The Fullness Of The Divine Will Of God. And God Has Given Us The Cure.

It Is Living In The Gift Of The Divine Will– Which Is the Source And Operative Life Of The Trinity - That Runs the Trinity!

It Is Our Responsibility To Learn About God's Gift For Our Time, Receive It, And Live In It.

The Greatest Explosion Of The Supernatural Is Being Poured Out In Our Time To Help Us.

God Is Providing The Gift Of The Divine Will From The Center Of The Trinity As Divine Help - And A Cure For Our Failing Condition, But There Is a

Mystery Around Luisa Piccarreta And God's Gift For Our Time, And Who Is Responding.

Jesus is Giving This Gift To Whom He Gives It To. Period. It Seems That Most People Don't Want To Know and Don't Want To Be Cured With God's Divine Gift.

Luisa Asked Jesus:

Why He Didn't Give This Great Gift Before.

And Jesus Explained To Her That That When He Came 2,000 Years Ago, People Were Not Ready To Receive This Divine Gift.

He Had To Take Us From The Lesser To The Greater Knowledge –
And Now We Are Ready To Receive This Gift.

God Is Offering Us The Sealing Of His Covenant.

Learning About This Gift Costs Us.
It Takes Our Time And Our Attention.
Our Time And Our Attention Are The Two Coins that
We Have To Spend Each Day.

We Must Learn About This Gift and The Great
Love That Jesus Has Prepared For Each Of Us–
He Died For Each Of Us– And He Is Offering Us The
Divine Will As Covenant.

This is The Fulfillment And The Completion Of
The New Covenant That God Has Prepared For
Each Of Us.
We Must Trust In God Completely To Accept This
Covenant.

**The Covenant Terms Is To Turn Over Our Human
Will To Him Completely– And For Him To Give
Himself To Us Completely– And Possess Us And**

**Take Over Complete Control Of Our Life –
This is God's Sealing Of The New Covenant On
Earth.**

You Are Either Completely In, Or Completely Out.
Jesus Wants Us To Live On Earth As In Heaven.
This Has Been His Plan From The Beginning.
It Has Begun!
God Is Marking Those For The Highest Places In
Heaven In The Divine Will- And Satan Has Been
Marking Those For Hell.

Humanity Is Not Going To Deal With Or Fix The
Problem Of The Descent Of Our Civilization Into
Chaos And Hell.

Humanity Has Run Into A Dead End!

And God Has Allowed This So That We Will
Finally Begin To Listen To The God Of Revelation
- Not Just The Book Of Revelation In The Bible But
All Of Revelation! God Has Been Revealing
Himself To Man – And Man To Man All Down

Human History But Few People Have Any Clue What God Is Telling Us!

The New Covenant

**Just When It Seems That All Is Lost –
The Gift Of The Divine Will Is The Fulfillment
And The Sealing Of The New Covenant!**

God Has Given Us The Great Gift Of The Divine Will To Cleanse Us And Prepare Us To Live In A New Era Of Peace For All Mankind.

Even As It Is Raining Sin And Death Upon The Earth, God Has Sent Out His Mother As The Sinless Ark – Mary Is The First Human Creature To Live Completely In The Divine Will – And We Can Now Enter Into The Sinless Ark. This Ark Is Sealed Against Sin And Death And Will Lift Us Up Above The Mud Of The World.

Lost Knowledge

Most Christians Do Not Know:

The New Covenant is The Two Step Process of Redemption and Sanctification.

We have been living The Redemption,
The Gift Of Living In The Divine Will Is The
Sanctification– We Are Made Holy.

The New Covenant

The New Covenant is the spiritual fulfillment of the Abrahamic Covenant.

Hebrews 8: 7-12 - KJV

"For if that First Covenant had been faultless, no other place would have been sought for the Second.

For finding fault with them, he saith, Behold the days come, sayeth the Lord, when I will make A New Covenant with the House of Israel and with the House of Judah; not according to the Covenant that I made with their fathers in the day when I took them by the hand to lead them out of the land of Egypt; because they continued not in my Covenant, and I regarded them not, sayeth the Lord.

For this is the Covenant that I will make with the house of Israel after those days, saith the Lord;

I will put my laws into their mind, and write them in their hearts: and I will be to them of God, and they shall be to me a people: And they shall not teach every man his neighbor, and every man his brother, saying, Know the Lord: for all shall know me, from the least to the greatest. For I will be merciful to their unrighteousness, and their sins and their iniquities will I remember no more.

In that he saith, A New Covenant, he hath made the first old. Now that which decayeth and waxeth old is ready to vanish away.

Christians believe that the new covenant was established at the last supper as part of the Eucharist, when Jesus said, this cup is the new covenant in my blood, which is poured out for you. Luke 22: 20

The New Covenant is a promise from God to forgive sin and restore fellowship with those who turn their hearts toward him.

Is mediated by Jesus Christ, and his death on the cross is the basis of this of the promise. The New Covenant provides God's power to live for him, and God gives His Holy Spirit to motivate and empower people to fulfill his moral instructions.

The New Covenant also promises that God will write His laws in people's hearts, sanctify them, and make them holy.

What is The New Covenant? The New Covenant is the promise that God will forgive sin and restore fellowship with those whose hearts are turned to him.

The Fulfillment

This Is The Fulfillment Of The New Covenant The Divine Will Is The Capstone Of The New Covenant.

The Three Appeals ... My Divine Will is the seed, the beginning, the means, the end and the coronation of Man, My Gospel, and My Church...

While Our Society Is Falling Down Around Us! And We Have Been Descending Down Into The Abyss – And Doors Have Been Are Closing Behind Us.

And People Ask: Where Are the Promises Of His Coming?

God Has Been Working Behind The Scenes Preparing His Greatest Triumph, And We Can All Be A Part Of It At The Divine Level!

The Problem With Humanity

The Problem With The Condition Of Humanity Is That We Have Been Living In A Fallen State Of Being- With Our Human Will Running Our Lives - Disconnected From The Divine Will.

We Were Not Meant For Our Human Will To Live Separate From The Divine Will.

The Human Will Is In A Spiritual Descent In Which The Doors Are Closing Behind Us.

The Gift Of The Divine Will Is Our Way Of Escape

Humanity Is Not Going To Deal With Or Fix The Problem Of The Descent Of Our Civilization Into Chaos And Hell.

Humanity Has Run Into A Dead End! And God Has Allowed This So That We Will Finally Begin To

Listen To The God Of Revelation - Not Just The Book Of Revelation In The Bible But All Of God's Revelation Down the History Of Man.

God Has Been Revealing Himself To Man - And Man To Man - All The Way Down Human History- But Few People Have Any Clue What God Is Telling Us- Or Where It Is All Leading Up To.

It All Leads Up To The Fulfillment And The Sealing Of The New Covenant.

Only God Can Intervene And Save Us- And That Intervention Is Happening In God's Gift Of Living In The Divine Will.

The Gift Of The Divine Will Is the Capstone Of The New Covenant.
All Of Human History Has Led Up To God Giving Us This Gift Of The Divine Will.

It All Leads To The New Covenant In Which God Brings Us Back Into His Kingdom.

All Of Human History Is The Story Of the Prodigal Son Leaving the Father And Returning Home.

The Basic Story Of Humanity

**People Forgot
The Basic Story Of God and Humanity!**

People Forgot That Jesus Is Coming Back To Claim
the Earth,
and Restore Us To The Way Adam and Eve Were
Before the Fall,
and That Satan Would Be Banished!

Adam and Eve Lost The Gift Of The Divine Will-
And Jesus Gave It Back To Us!

People Forgot About Adam and Eve -Our First
Parents

- and that We Are All Living In A Fallen Nature-

And The Promises Of The Old And New
Testaments:

Are That The Messiah Would Restore All Things
To the Way They Were In The Garden Of Eden
Before The Fall.

**This Is What Jesus Came To Do! This Is The
Fulfillment Of The Old And The New Covenant!
This Is The Gift Of The Divine Will!**

All Of Luisa's Writings Are Dictated By Jesus Who
Lived In Her And Wants To Live In Us And Do All
Our Acts Too!

This Is How Adam and Eve Lived Before The Fall.
God's Promises Of The New Covenant Are Fulfilled
In The Gift Of Living In The Divine Will.

Create in me a pure heart, O God, and renew a
steadfast spirit within me.

Psalm 51:10

332

Do not conform to the pattern of this world, but be transformed by the renewing of your mind.
Then you will be able to test and approve what God's Will is – His Good, Pleasing and Perfect Will.

Romans 12:2

Central Message

The Central Message Of Jesus To Luisa is Love and Mercy For Us No Matter What Our Condition God is Fixing Our Problems And Giving A New Start For Humanity. To Live A New and Higher Divine Life With God.

As St. Augustin Taught:
God Will Not Fix Our Problems Without Our Cooperation!

"New And Divine Holiness"

This "New And Divine Holiness" is Now Available And It Is Simple and Easy To Do, To The Degree That We Are Willing To Make The Greatest Of Sacrifices, To Not Do Our Human Will Anymore, Or Have It Have Life On Its Own In Us.

The Central Problem With The Human Condition Is That We Are Living In A Defective Fallen Nature and God Has Given Us The Cure- The Fix.

The Issue Now That God Has Given Us The Cure For Our Sinful Condition Is To Get People To Learn What The Problem Is and What The Cure Is- The Cure Is Called Living In The Gift Of The Divine Will. All We Have To Do Is Learn About It, Receive It, And Live In It.

Nothing else is needed but to make It known.

Book Of Heaven - September 16,1928

..." See then, my daughter, everything is ready- nothing else is needed but to make It known. And this is why i so much yearn that what regards my Divine Will become known- to cast into creatures the desire to possess a good so great, so that my Will, drawn by their desires, concentrate its luminous rays and, with Its heat, perform the prodigy of giving them back the right to possess Its Kingdom of peace, of happiness and of sanctity."

Major Cataclysmic Destruction And Then The Era Of Peace.

You Tube Shorts @ElijahsCloak

Divine Will – Fulfillment Of Creation That's what the Third Fiat is about.

"The Gift of the Divine Will is not just a Gift for man, it is a Gift for all of Creation. The Third Fiat presents us with the promise of a New Heaven and a New Earth; and it explains what Saint Paul"

The Great Event

The Great Event is Coming
The Middle Coming All Builds Up To The Era Of

Book Of Heaven – Volume 15– July 14, 1923

The Paternal Goodness Wants To Open Another Era Of Grace

Preparations for the war and threats of chastisements. Through Luisa, they will be reduced by half.

Awaiting The New Era. Expectation Of A New Era …

Jesus to Luisa:

"… afterwards, He added: My daughter, the whole world is upside down, everyone is waiting for changes, for peace, for new things.

They even gather to discuss about it, but they are surprised at not being able to conclude anything and come up with serious decisions. So true peace does not arise, and everything comes up to words, but no facts. And they hope that more conferences may serve to take serious decisions, but they wait in vain.

In the meantime, in this waiting, they are all fearful and some get ready for new wars, some hope for new conquest.

But with this, peoples are impoverished and are stripped alive; While they are waiting, tired of the sad era, which, dark and bloody, enwraps them, they wait and hope for A New Era Of Peace and of Light ...”

“The world is exactly at the same stage when I was about to come upon earth.

All were awaiting a great event, a New Era; as it indeed occurred. The same now; **Since the great Event is coming- the New Era in which the Will of God will be done on earth as it is in Heaven-**

everyone is waiting for this new Era, being tired of the present one, but not knowing what this novelty, this change is, just as they did not know it when I came upon the earth.

This wait is a sure sign that the hour is near. **But the most certain sign is that I am manifesting what I want to do; And turning to a soul, just as I turned to my Mama** in descending from Heaven I communicate to her My Will and the goods and effects it contains, **in order to give It as Gift to all humanity."**

This Divine Will is not that hard.

You just have to call Jesus Into doing all your acts.

Everything you do – you do in the Divine Will. And the Benefits are Divine and Amazing!

This Gift Is Not Difficult To Understand! I Am Explaining the Basics To You In My Book, And Now That You Know About The Luisa Piccarreta And the Gift Of The Divine Will, Then All You Have To Do Is To Keep Learning About It, and Sign Yourself Over To This Gift And Jesus Will Enter Into You And Do All Your Acts And Take Over Running Your Life!

You Know Enough Already To Give Your Yes To This Gift!

You Give your Yes And Sign Yourself Over To Jesus' Doing All Your Acts And He Takes You At

Your Word and Takes Over Full Control Of Your Life. You Keep Learning About The Divine Will And Are Drawn In Completely.

Be Careful Because the Divine Will Is Divinely Powerful. You Sign Yourself Over Unto Death. You Are Signing Yourself Over To Be Cleansed and Stripped Of All Your Human Attachments.

This Is The Sinless Ark Of The Covenant, The Blessed Virgin Mary Herself That We Are Entering. Remember Uzzah Was Struck Dead For Just Touching The Ark Of The Covenant – That Foretold Mary The True Ark Of The True Living Covenant.

Our Lady Is Our Divine Will Refuge. Our Lady's Greatest Title Is "Queen and Mother Of The Divine Will."

Jesus told Luisa To Be Careful How You Speak About The Divine Will; God Himself Is Controlling these Writings and Who Is Receiving Them.

Living With The Human Will Alone Running Our Lives Is Coming To An End.

Only Those Living In The Divine Will Survive The Change Coming Over The Earth.

We Need Gods Supernatural Power To Weather The Spiritual Battle That Has Overtaken The Earth!

The Gift Of Living In The Divine Will Is Our Refuge And Spiritual Vehicle For Our Sanctification:

The Demon Is Being Vanquished And Chained For 1,000 Years.

This Is The Middle Coming Of Jesus All Building Up To The Era of Peace.

This Is The Millennium Of Peace That Is What All The History Of Humanity Has Built Up To.

It Is Only At The End Of the Millennium Of Peace That Satan Will Be Released For A Short

Time and Then Jesus Will Return for The Definitive Second Coming For The Final Judgement, and It Will Be Heaven Or Hell For Eternity.

All Humans Are Being Recreated In The Image And Likeness Of God That Adam And Eve Lived Before The Fall.

We Are Coming Through Purification In Which Most Of This Generation Will Be Destroyed, And The Few Survivors Will Live In An Era Of Peace In Which Paradise And The Earth Are Joined.

The Bible Promises For The Millenium Of Peace:
"Blessed are the meek, for they shall inherit the earth." (Mathew 5:5 KJV)

"For Behold, I create New Heavens and a New Earth; And the former things shall not be remembered or come to mind.

Be glad and rejoice forever in that which I create; for behold, I create Jerusalem a rejoicing, and her people a joy.

I will rejoice in Jerusalem, and be glad in my people; No more shall be heard in it the sound of weeping and the cry of distress.

No more shall there be in it an infant that lives but a few days, or an old man who does not fill out his days, for the child shall die a hundred years old, and the sinner being a hundred years old shall be accursed.

They shall build houses and inhabit them; They shall plant vineyards and eat their fruit. They shall not build and another inhabit; They shall not plant and another eat; for like the days of a tree shall the days of my people be, and my chosen shall long enjoy the work of their hands.

The wolf and the lamb shall feed together, the lion shall eat straw like the ox and dust shall be the serpent's food.

They shall not hurt or destroy in all my holy mountain, says the Lord."

(Isaiah 65 RSV 17-22, 25)

The First Resurrection

This is the most blessed time to ever be alive, for we are coming through the Great Purification, and then into the Glorious Era Of Peace upon the earth,

The Thousand Year Reign Of God On Earth– The Glorious Era Of Peace

Revelation 20:1-4 RSV

Then I saw an Angel coming down from Heaven, holding in his hand the key of the bottomless pit and a great chain.

And he seized the dragon, that ancient serpent, who was the devil and bound him for 1,000 years, and threw him into the pit, and shut it and sealed it over him, that he should deceive the nations no more, till the 1,000 years were ended. After that he must be loosed for a little while.

Revelation 20: 4-6 RSV

Then I saw Thrones, and sealed on them were those to whom judgment was committed.

Also I saw the souls of those who had been beheaded for their testimony to Jesus and for the word of God, and who had not worshipped the beast or its image and had not received its mark on their forehead or their hands. They came to life and reigned with Christ for 1,000 years.

The Rest Of The Dead Did Not Come To Life Until The Thousand Years Were Ended.

This is The First Resurrection.

Blessed and Holy is he who shares in The First Resurrection!

Over such The Second Death has no power, but they shall be priests of God and of Christ, and They Shall Reign With Him 1,000 years.

Revelation 20: 7-10 RSV

And when the 1,000 years are ended, Satan will be loosed from his prison and will come out to deceive the nations which are at the four corners of the earth, that is, Gog and Magog, to gather them for battle; their number is like the sand of the sea.

The Final Judgement And The Second Coming Only At The End Of The Millennium Of Peace.

Revelation 20:11 RSV

Then I saw A Great White Throne and Him who sat upon it; From His Presence earth and sky fled away, and no place was found for them, and you and I saw the dead, great and small, Standing Before The Throne, and Books Were Opened.

Another book was opened which is The Book Of Life, and the dead were judged by what was written in the books, by what they had done. And the sea gave up the dead in it, Death and Hades gave up the dead in them, and All Were Judged By What They Had Done.

Then Death and Hades were thrown into The Lake Of Fire. This is The Second Death, The Lake Of Fire; And If Anyone's Name Was Not Found Written In The Book Of Life, He Was Thrown Into The Lake Of Fire.

Our Father's World

This Is Our Father's World And The Entire World Is Being Cleansed

The Divine Will Is The Cowning Glory Of Our Humanity – Which Was Originally Connected And Diffused Into Our Human Will.

Instead Adam And Eve Pulled Their Human Will Out Of The Fullness Of The Divine Will And Left Us To Our Own Devices.

Now God Is Bringing Us Into The Promised Land – The Era Of Peace

God Promised That The Messiah Would Restore The Spiritual Gifts That Adam And Eve Lost And That Includes The Paradise Of The Garden Of Eden Upon The Earth

Fr. Celso Tells Us To Quit Complaining And Be Happy

Padre Pio Told Us: "Pray And Don't Worry."

In Placing Our Human Will Back Into The Divine Will, We Have A Place To Rest, And Where God Could Rest In Us –

And God Would Have A Place To Operate In And Through Us In Complete Freedom.

Book Of Heaven - Volume 12- February 27,1919 Jesus to Luisa:

"It will Be the Era Of True Liberty: Liberty of the Creature To Take All That is of Jesus

"...Oh, what free vent my Love will have! I will have a free field in everything, no longer hindered. I will have as many tabernacles as I wish; the Hosts will be innumerable.

At each instant We will communicate together and even I will cry out: Freedom. Freedom! Everyone come into My Will to enjoy true Liberty! Outside of my Will, how many hinderances does the soul not find.

But in My Will is liberty. I leave her free to love Me as she wishes. Indeed, I say to her: "Leave your human spoils; take the divine. I am not stingy or jealous of my goods. I want you to take everything..."

Two Ways To Live

There Are Only Two Ways To Live, And We Have All Been Living The Way That We Were Born Into, And The Only Way We Have Known How To Live,

And That Is The Way That All Human Beings Have Been Living For All Of Human History–

But That Way Of Living Is Coming To An End–

We Have Been Living In A Fallen Defective Nature, With Our Human Will Running Our Lives– But That Is Coming To An Abrupt Halt.

The Earth Is Changed. We Are Coming Into Cataclysmic Changes Upon The Earth.

It's a Purification, And A Cleansing Of The Earth.

We Cannot Survive The Cataclysmic Changes Coming Over The Earth Living With Your Human Will Running Your Life.

We Need The Divine Will To Take Over Operating
Control Of Your Life.

Known History

This Coincides With Known Human History

Mankind As We Know It, Just Appeared On Earth 6,000 Years Ago, And Since Then Satan Has Been The Lord Of The World.

We May Not Have Been Explicitly Possessed By Satan, But Some Did And Do Go That Far To Use Their Free Will To Consent to The Demon Living and Running Their Lives.

The Demon Cannot Fully Possess A Human Being, It's Always An Uncomfortable Fit But They Will Certainly Try.

Only God Can Perfectly Possess A Human Being Completely- And That's How Human Beings Are Designed And Created For- To Be Perfect Habitations Of God.

We Live At The End Of The Era Of Human Disobedience And Of The Reign Of Satan Upon The Earth.

This Is Accomplished Through Living In The Gift Of The Divine Will – Which Is The Middle Coming Of Jesus. And This All Culminates In The Millennium Of Peace For The Whole World.

Satan Is Being Chained For A Thousand Years, And Only Then At The End Of The Thousand Years Will Satan Be Released For A Short Time To Seek Those Whom To Enter Into;

Then Comes The Definitive And Official Second Coming Of Jesus.

It's The Final Judgement And Then It's Heaven Or Hell For Eternity.

An Era

An Era Is A 2,000 Year Period

Jesus Tells Us That Every 2,000 Year Period Is A Purification.

In The First 2,000-year Period Was A Physical Purification Of The Deluge.
Then The Spiritual Purification In The Redemption.

And Now The Purification By Fire In Which Most Of This Generation Like "Noxious Plants" Will Be Destroyed.

Book Of Heaven - July 21, 1900,

Necessity Of Purification

And He [Jesus]: "It is necessary, absolutely, for the sake of purgation in every place, because in the field sowed by Me weeds and thorns have grown so much as to become trees.

And these thorny trees do nothing but inundate my field with poisonous and pestilent waters, to the point that if some ear of grain remains intact, it receives nothing but punctures and stench, so much so, that it is impossible for more ears to germinate

– First, because they lack the ground, which is occupied by so many noxious plants;

Second, because of the continuous punctures they receive, which give them no peace.

So, behold the necessity of the slaughter – to root out so many bad plants; and of shedding of blood –

to purge my field of these of those poisonous and pestilent waters.

Therefore do not want to grow sad at this beginning, because not only there where I have sent chastisements, but in all other places is purgation needed."

Jesus Tells Us: The Survivors Will Be Few.

They Will Be The Remnant Which Will Live A Renewed Existence And Repopulate The Earth.

This Is Accomplished In Those Taking Up Living In Gift Of The Divine Will.

God Is Pouring Out The Very Source And The Operative Power From The Center Of The Trinity – That Runs The Trinity – Now Into Having Operating Life Into Us.

This Power Is Multiplied To The Infinite And Magnified In Us And Restores All Humanity Past, Present, And Future To The Degree That They Can Receive It And Restores The Universe.

This Blessing Returns To Us And We Give The Divine Will As A Return Of Love To The Father And

He Receives All The Glory Due Him As If Mankind Had Never Fallen,

And All Had Been Done In The Divine Will And Gave The Proper Return Of Love To The Father.

It Is Right And Just That The Father Receive All the Glory That He should Have Received As If Angels and Humans Had Never Fallen, And All Had Been Done In The Divine Will.

And When The Full Measure Of Glory To The Father Is Reached, There Will Be A Manifestation Of The Era Of Peace Upon The Earth.

All this Happens In Those Living In The Divine Will.

The Demon Has No Power Over Those In The Divine Will.

God Can Sanctify Us, As We Take The Divine Will On Loan And Give God All Rights Over Us.

A New And Higher Life Is Being Given To All Humans Who Will Turn Over Their Lives To God In The Divine Will.

The Past 6,000 Year Period Is Ending.

We Live In A Transition Not Just From One Era To Another But A Change Of Age To A New Era Of Peace.

We Humans Have Been Prey Of Demons Who Have Been Able To Cause Problems For Us, And Twist And Turn The Human Wills To Their Own Use. But, If You Know The Bible, And Are Able To Follow The History Of God's Revelation To Humans- And His Purposes To Amend Our Defective Nature, Then You Would Be Able To Follow All Of God's Revelation History To Humans Right Up To God Giving Us Back The Gift Of The Divine Will To Humanity.

Jesus Gave The Gift To Luisa On September 8,1889, And Then Dictated The 36 Volumes Of The Book Of Heaven Which Is The Instruction Manual

For How Humans Are To Receive And Live In The Divine Will For The Rest Of Our Life On Earth And Then For Eternity In Heaven.

It Is All Gift. But We Have To Learn About It, Receive It And Live In It.

We Have Come To The Promised Time.

The Bible Teaches That There Was To Come A Time On Earth, When God Would Reclaim Human Beings And The Earth, And That Is What God Is Doing Right Now In The Gift Of Living In The Divine Will.

It Is Now Happening In The Gift Of Living In The Divine Will.

God Is Recreating Humans Beings In Those Who Are Taking Up Living In The Gift Of The Divine Will. And God Is Using Those In The Divine Will To Send His Graces Into Them- And Renewing Nature And The Earth. This Is God's Big Plan And We Are So Blessed To Be The Generation

That Is Called Upon To Take Up Living In The Divine Will.

If You understand The Times We Live In Then You Realize That The Divine Will Is Promised For Our Time. All Of Human History Has Been Prelude To And Preparation For God To Give This Gift And For Us Humans Now Alive To Partake Of This Restoration Of Humanity And Of The World.

God is reclaiming the earth after 6000 years of human existence.

It's been 6000 years in which has been the time of the disobedience, and now is the restoration of humanity and of the earth.

[The 6,000 Year Time Frame Is A Stumbling Block For Some, But It Shouldn't Be. This Coincides With Known Human History. About 6,000 Years Human Beings as We Know them Just Appeared On the Earth, Able to Transmit Their History Down To Us In Writing.] [We Can Speculate What Came Before- We Are Not Told-

But There Were Bipedal Hominids- And The Bible Mentions Fallen Angels Or Giants] In the Gift of the Divine Will Satan is Vanquished, And Humans Are Lifted Up.   People Who Have Followed God's Gifts Of Salvation Down Revelation History - Realize That All Of Human History – And All Of Revelation History All Builds Up To God Giving The Gift Of The Divine Will For The Healing Of Humanity- And The Cleaning Up Of The Church For The Wedding Feast – Which Is The Era Of Peace Being Granted To The Whole Earth.

Simple Explanation

A Simple Explanation Of The Divine Will God's Divine Will That We Are Talking About Is The Actual Source And Operative Life Of The Trinity.

All Three Persons Of The Trinity Hold The Divine Will In Common.

On the pamphlet the Kingdom of The Divine Will – Copyright 1995 The Luisa Piccarreta Center of the Divine Will.

Fiat!

"Dearly beloved of God, We would like to introduce you to a very beautiful story about God and His Divine Will and how the Divine Will wishes to reign on earth as it does in heaven; For the time has now arrived.

In the beginning, before all Creation came into being, was God. God is a Trinity of Persons: Father, Son, and Holy Spirit. Their Persons are distinct; yet They are a perfect unity of oneness in Being, Essence, and Will.

The highest and most beautiful thing that can be said of Them is that they have but one Will among Themselves; thus, there is the most perfect unity, harmony, peace and delight.

With the infinite power of this Divine Will, the three Divine Persons continually produce new and increasing joys and happiness and delights among themselves.

Their Kingdom is Their Divine Will, the same Kingdom that we pray to come on earth when we recite the Lord's Prayer.

It is Life – pure Life – the very Vital Principle of the Holy Trinity. One God. This Kingdom Of The Divine Will produces everything for God.

It produces all the attributes, the perfections, joys, delights, and happiness of the Holy Trinity."

This Gift

This Same Kingdom That Reigns In The Trinity Is Now Being Given To Everyone, In The Gift Of The Divine Will.

This Same Divine Will Which Runs The Trinity Is Designed In Our Creation To Have Operational Control Of Our Human Lives And Run Our Souls And Our Lives.

Thus we Would Have The Harmony That The Trinity Has Within It, And Be Part Of Its Intimate Inner Life.

Now God Is Offering Us A New And A Higher Divine Life - That Is, The Gift Of Living In The Divine Will. This Is - The Gift Of Our Lady As Refuge And Sinless Ark Of The Covenant - For Us To Enter Into And To Live A New And Divine Holiness.

God had to let us all have broken hearts, and we all see how evil is; and how our society is just becoming more and more evil and filthy, and we've all been part of it.

This has Happened On Our Watch, And We Are All Responsible and Will Stand Before God

But God Has Allowed All This So That We Will Finally Turn Over Our Lives To His Plan- To Take Over Running Our Lives Completely- And Fix all Our Problems- With Our Total Acceptance And Cooperation.

A New Phase

A New Phase Of The Spiritual Battle

This Spiritual Battle Is Raging On –

But Is Entering A New Phase-

The Reign Of The Divine Will On Earth As It Is In Heaven.

This Is The Spiritual Battle- That Each Of Us Is Responsible For Entering Into And Living In The Divine Will.

The Importance Of Our Acts Done In The Divine Will:

God Is Relying On Us Humans To Live In And To Do Our Acts In The Divine Will. This Is How God Is Winning The Victory.

**Humans Living In The Divine Will
Defeats The Human Will–**

**Sanctifies Human Beings,
Brings About The Era Of Peace
And Vanquishes Satan.**

The Army

God Provides The Army - Which Is The Knowledge Of The Divine Will –

The Weapons Of Light

But God Is Relying On Those Living In The Divine Will To Provide The Weapons. Those Weapons Are Our Acts Done In The Divine Will.

These Are Weapons Of Light

Between Us And God –One On One – -But Each Of Us Involves Everyone – All Are Affected by the Outcome.

To Defeat The Human Will, Usher In The Era Of Peace, And Most Of All, To Give A Return Of Love To The Father.

Human Will

Our Lady Explains The Human Will

The Blessed Virgin Mary Explained The Human Will And The Divine Will To Luisa In the Book:

'The Virgin Mary in the Kingdom of the Divine Will' by Luisa... the Little Daughter of the Divine Will.

The Center for the Divine Will Jacksonville, FL 32210 Copyright 1996.

Our Lady explains what the human will is on its own.

Day Four: Lessons Of The Queen Of Heaven ...

"Child of my heart, pay attention to Me: it is My Heart of Mother which wants to pour itself out to her child.

I want to tell you my secrets which until now I have not revealed to anyone because the hour of God had not yet sounded.

God has wanted to bestow surprising grace is upon creatures which in all the history of the world He has not conceded to anyone.

He wants to make known the prodigies of the Divine Fiat and what It can do in the creature if it lets itself be dominated by It, Therefore He wants to place as model in the sight of everyone, Me, who had the great honor of forming my life all of Divine Will."

Day Five

Now, listen to Me, dear child: as the Supreme Being asked of me my human will, I understood the grave evil that the human will can do in the creature and how it puts everything into danger, even the most beautiful works of its Creator.

The creature, with its human will, is all vacillating, weak, and constant, disordered. And this is so because God, in creating it, created it united as in nature with His Divine Will in such a way that it should be the strength, the prime movement, the support, the food, the life of the human will.

Thus, by not giving life to the Divine Will in ours, the goods received from God in the Creation are rejected and also the rights received in nature in the act in which we were created.

Oh, how I understood well the grave offense which is made to God and the evils which pour down upon the creature! I had such horror and fear of doing my will that justly I feared, because Adam also was created innocent by God; yet, by doing his will, into how many evils did not he and all generations plunge?

(When we are living in The Divine Will, we only have one will – which is God's Divine Will. The human will is completely dominated and operated by the Divine Will.)

Prevenient Offering

A Prevenient Offering Is A Morning Offering For The Full Day - or any offering of yourself for a certain period- like an offering before sleeping.

You Choose Your Prayer But It Must Include This: To Call Jesus Into Doing All Your Acts.

You Call Jesus Into Doing All Your Acts - In The Divine Will.

Thus You Call The Divine Will Into Possessing And Directing All Your Acts- Body And Soul - and You Constantly Give To God Your Freedom To Say YES! – FIAT! Fiat! Let It Be Done To Me According To Your Good Pleasure – Your Divine Will.

You Offer Yourself Up At The Beginning Of The Day In What Is Called A Prevenient" Prayer Offering And Then All Day Long In Continual "Actual" Offerings.

God Wants Us To Be Faithful and Attentive To Doing All Our Acts In The Divine Will.

Here Is A Short Prevenient Prayer Come Supreme Will:

Come Supreme Will,

Come To Reign Upon The Earth,

Come To Reign In Me.

And Here Is A Short Prayer To Pray All Day Long As We Are Doing All Our Acts:

Jesus, You Do It In Me

Or

Jesus, You Do All My Acts In Me,

Calling All Souls To Be Disposed To Receive The
Divine Will,

All For The Glory Of The Father.

God Is Raising Us Up

God Is Reclaiming The Earth And Vanquishing Satan In The Gift Of Living In The Divine Will.

The Wonders of God Never Left Off In The Redemption.

They Have Continued Onward In The Story of God's Sanctification. and Now, Let Us Together Plumb The Depths Of The Interior Divine Wonders That God Is Pouring Out In Our Time!

This Divine Will is not that hard! You just have to call Jesus into doing everything that you do - in the Divine Will.

It Is A Divine Indwelling And the Benefits are Divine!

The Gift

Luisa Received The Gift Of The Divine Will.

Adam And Eve Lived In The Divine Will Before Their Fall.

Jesus and Mary Both Lived In The Divine Will On Earth And For All Eternity.

Of Course Jesus Is God and He Always Lived In The Divine Will.

All Three Persons Of The Trinity Always Lived In The Divine Will.

Mary Was Sinless and Lived In The Divine Will All Her Life.

Luisa Was Conceived And Born With The Original Sin- And She Is The First Person With Original Sin To Enter Into The Divine Will.

This Gift Was Given To Luisa For Her and For All Humans. We have To Just Learn About It, Receive It, and Live In It.

Available To Everyone

This Gift Is Available To Everyone One Earth!

book of heaven.com

Luisa's Mystical Marriage and Gift of the Divine Will.

Nativity of The Blessed Virgin Mary Luisa Receives The Gift Of Living in the Divine Will September 8, 1889, Feast of the Nativity of Mary.

Luisa's Mystical Marriage Renewed.

Book Of Heaven– Volume One

"I saw that the Most Holy Trinity Descended into my heart and took Possession of it- and there, They Formed Their Dwelling.

Who can tell the change that occurred in me? I felt Divinized; It was no longer I who lived, but They were Living in me."

Book Of Heaven–

Volume 13– December 5, 1921.

The Gift of the Divine Will was given to Luisa from the time of the Renewal of Mystical Marriage before the Holy Trinity, 32 years before.

Luisa To Jesus:

"Tell me my life, who is my family? What is my dowry and yours?

Jesus To Luisa:

And smiling, He continued: "Your family is the Trinity. Don't you remember that in the first years of bed I took you to Heaven and we celebrated our Union before the Most Holy Trinity?

It endowed you with such Gifts that you yourself have not yet known; And as I speak to you about My Will, about its Effects and Value, and make you discover the Gifts with which, from time to time, you were endowed.

I do not speak to you about My Dowry, because what is Mine is yours.

And then after a few days, We the Three Divine Persons descended from Heaven, took possession of your heart, and Formed our Perpetual Residence in it.

We took the Reins of your intelligence, of your heart, and all of yourself;

And everything you did was an Outpouring of Our Creative Will over you, and confirmation that your human will was animated by an Eternal Will.

The work is already done. There Is nothing left but to make It Known, so that, not only you but others may take part in these Great Goods.

And this I am doing by calling now one minister, now another, and even some places apart, to make known to them these great truths.

Therefore, this thing is mine- not yours; so, let me do. Even more, you must know that every time you manifest one additional value of My Will, I feel so much contentment that I love you with multiplied love.

THE VALUE OF LUISA'S FIAT

Book of Heaven – Volume 20– 9/11/24

"My daughter, remember that I asked of you a "Yes" in My Will, and you (Luisa) pronounced it with all love.

That "Yes" still exists and holds its prime place in My unending Will.

Everything you (Luisa) do, think and say, is bound to that "Yes", which nothing can escape, and My Will enjoys and makes feast in seeing a will of creature Live In My Will; and I keep filling her with New Graces, making all of your acts Divine Acts.

This is the greatest portent which exists between Heaven and earth. It Is the object most dear to Me..."

The Value Of Our Fiat.

"A New And Divine Life" is now available to everyone.

God's Kingdom Is Coming To Earth In Those Who Are Receiving The Greatest Gift That God Can Ever Give Creatures- Even In Heaven!

And There Are Special Benefits To Receiving This On Earth.

Now That Luisa Gave Her Yes, and Received This Gift,

We Can All Give Our Yes And Receive This Gift.

This Gift Is The Kingdom Of God Coming Down Into Human Beings.
This Is Our Time Of Decision!

Its Get In the Ark Of The Covenant Or Stay Outside!

"THE GIFT OF GIFTS"

The Following Is Quoted From A Divine Will Meeting Of Fr. John O. Brown, One Of "The Original Divine Will Priests."

Quoted From You Tube Video
Fr. John O Brown Continuous Act Of Being Reborn

@ **Divine Will– Queen Of Light Cenacle Speaking Of The Fourth Degree:**

Fr. John O. Brown:
"...God introduces us to the Divine Will and He says: "... But that's where the Divine Merit is gained, and if there's something holding you back – if you have something that's [or] even your own thinking saying that's not for me – I could never do that, I can't arrive at that, then you are talking yourself out of the Greatest Gift that God ever gave you and that's exactly what you're doing:

You are talking yourself out of one of the simplest things there is to give - "an act of consent" to what God wants to offer and He wants to offer you the Gift of The Divine Will' It is the "Gift of all Gifts" that has ever been given by God since the Creation of the World,

and He said, I want you to grow in it to drive at a point, but I want you to get to that point where you become something different, something else, **you become transubstantiated to become not human but a Life in the [Divine] Sun, and I want that Life to be Perfectly Perpetuating in you and the only way that can happen is for you to live in The Eternal Now,**

To be able to say Fiat! Fiat! Fiat! every moment regardless of What God is bringing you - ..." you don't judge what God is bringing you."

Jesus Explains The Human Will

Jesus told Luisa that the human will holds no attraction for Him outside of the Divine Will.

Book Of Heaven – January 31, 1928
Luisa To Jesus:

"After this I was thinking of how much evil the human will has done to poor creatures, hence I abhorred, I neither want to know it anymore, nor to look at it because it is too nauseating, but while I thought of this,

my beloved Jesus moved in my interior and said to me:

"My daughter, the human will by itself is nauseating, but united with mine it is the most beautiful thing I created, more so that the Divinity was never able to bring forth a thing created by us that might make nausea, she united with ours would hold the continuous motion of goods, of light, of sanctity, of beauty,

and with our continuous motion that never ceases it would have been the greatest prodigy of the creation, our motion would purify her from every shadow of stain,

it would happen as to the seed, that, because it continually murmurs and holds its perennial motion, its waters are pure and crystalline, oh!"

Our Fallen Nature

We Do Not Realize That Our Fallen Nature Is All Pervasive.

As An Aside, On the Internet There Is Both A Priest And A Pastor Who Had Near Death Experiences (NDE) and Found Themselves In Hell. Jesus Told Them That They Had Lived For Themselves Alone And They Were Shocked! God Did Give Them A Second Chance!)

THERE IS A SPECIFIC TIMELINE

Many Scholars Agree:

A.D. 30 Is The Year of Jesus' Passion and Resurrection;

So That Means 2,000 Years From The Crucifixion And the Resurrection is Spring Of the Year 2030.

There is specific timeline folks!

All Cycles Of History All Culminate In This Time.

What Jesus told Luisa Piccarreta about the timeline:

Book Of Heaven – Volume 12 – January 29, 1919

Jesus To Luisa:

"My beloved daughter, I want you to know the order of my Providence. "In every 2,000- year period I have renewed the world."

(please see the chapter: "Jesus Explains The Times" for a fuller quote)

We Know the Purification Is Coming And then The Era Of Peace, Which Is What We Are All Waiting For.

We Are In The Birth Pangs, And The Era Of Peace Is Another Birth Of Christ On The Earth.

Here Is A Look At The Following Non-Fiction Book To Let You Know The Exact Date Of Jesus' Crucifixion Was 2,000 Years Ago.

Look At when the Crucifixion was. There is a Consensus That The Best Scholars Tell Us that Jesus lived on Earth 5 BC to 30 AD.
From The Book: *The Diary Of Jesus*,
A Preeminent First Century Scholar
Author: Jean Aulagnier

From the back cover of The Diary Of Jesus:

The author, a staunch Catholic, is a graduate from L'ecole Polytechnique, the most prestigious scientific school in France.

He is rigorous and precise in his scientific analysis.... For several years now, the author it's been all his free time researching the history of God's relationship with the human race.

In his research, he has concentrated on the 1st century of Christianity.

That Jesus was born in 5 BC is rather solidly established by historical data concerning – the census in Palestine – the fact that Jesus was exactly 30 when he began His Public Ministry – that Jesus' Public Ministry took place from AD 27 to AD 30 (P, 336)

At this point I must turn my attention to Jesus' birthday. .... I have mentioned previously that Jesus was born during the night of Tuesday, December 12th to Wednesday, December 13th

Julian in 5 BC in connection with the full moon of Teveth. (p. 346)

A.D. 30. The year of Jesus' Passion and Resurrection April 5 (Friday) This was now the day before Passover. (p. 336)

And We Know that- The Birth And Then the Crucifixion Of Jesus- Was Predicted and Happened When all The Cycles Of History All Coincided Down To The Exact Moment.
To Give You a Glimpse Of This- See On You Tube, The Movie: "The Star Of Bethlehem."
2007 Documentary/History by Frederick A. "Rick" Larson.

JESUS EXPLAINS THE TIMES

We Are Living In The Time Of A Purification – And Then A New Era Of Peace. This Is The purging of the earth and the destruction of a large part of the present generation.

Again: This is The Most Blessed Time To Ever Be Alive – If You Enter Into *The* Gift Of The Divine Will.

Here Are Two Quotes *From* The Book Of Heaven In Which Jesus Tells Us The Timeline Of Human History.

Book Of Heaven – January 29, 1919

Jesus To Luisa: "My beloved daughter, I want you to know the order of my Providence. In every 2,000– year period I have renewed the world."

"In the first period I renewed it with the Flood.

In the second 2,000 years, I renewed it with my coming to *the* earth and manifesting my Humanity from which, as so many channels of light, my Divinity shone.

And in this third period of 2,000 years, those who are good, and the Saints *themselves* have lived the fruit of my humanity, but have enjoyed my Divinity scarcely at all.

Now we are at the end of the third period and there will be a third renovation.

This is why there is general confusion. It is due to the preparation for the third renovation.

"And if in the second renovation I have manifested what my Humanity did and suffered, little was said about the working of my Divinity."

"Now in this third renovation after the purging of the earth and the destruction of a large part of the present generation, I will be still more generous with creatures."

"I will complete the renovation by manifesting what my Divinity did in my humanity, *how* my Divine Will worked with my Human Will, how everything remained joined in Me, how I did and redid everything, and even the thoughts of each creature were redone by me and sealed with my Divine Will."

"My Love wishes to release itself and make known the excesses that my Divinity worked in

my Humanity for creatures."

"These excesses greatly surpassed those which my humanity visibly worked. This is why I often speak to you about living in My Will which I have not manifested to anyone until now."

"At most they have known the shadow of My Will, the grace, the enchantment and sweetness that it contains."

"But to penetrate within, to embrace its immensity, to multiply oneself with Me, to penetrate everywhere, even while on earth, to penetrate into Heaven and into Hearts, to abandon human ways and work with Divine ways... This is not yet known."

"And this is so true that it will appear strange to many, and whoever does not have his mind open to the light of the truth will understand nothing.

"But little by little, I will make my way, manifesting at different times truths about my Will in such manner

that they will finally understand."

393

THE DEMONS LOSE THEIR KINGDOM

The Writings Of The Divine Will – Will Cause The Demons To Lose Their Kingdom On the Earth.

Book Of Heaven – September 22, 1924,

Luisa To Jesus:

"I continue: While I was writing what was said before, I saw my sweet Jesus who placed his mouth upon my heart.

His Breath inspired me with the words I was writing. And in those same moments I heard a horrible commotion at a distance, as though people were fighting and beating each other.

They howled with such a noise that it was frightening. Then, directing myself to my Jesus I said to Him: my Jesus, my Love who are they that are making such a commotion? They seem like furious demons. What do they want that *they* are fighting each other so much?

<u>*And Jesus: "My daughter, indeed they are demons. They do not want you to write about my Will because when they see you write the most important truths about living in my Will, they suffer double hell which torments the damned even more.*</u>

<u>*They are so afraid that these writings will be published about my Will and that their Kingdom on the earth will be lost.*</u>

<u>*This is the Kingdom acquired by them when man, withdrawing from my Divine Will, gave free reign to his human will.*</u>

Oh yes it was precisely then that the enemy acquired his reign on the earth.

But in the presence of My Will, the enemy will imprison himself in the deepest abysses.

This is why they fight with such fury. They feel the power of my will in these writings. Due to the possibility they could be published, they become furious and try with all their power to hinder such a great blessing. But don't pay attention to them; and because of this, learn to appreciate more my teachings..."

The Demons Know Their Time Is Short.

It is intriguing that the demons know their time is short and The Bible tells us that they seek to change the set times and the seasons.

Daniel 7:25 RSV

"He shall speak words against the Most High and shall wear out the saints of the Most High and shall think to change the times and the law; and they shall be given into his hand for a time, two times, and a half a time."

But the demons are not successful; and The Woman gives birth to the child – The New Generation Of Light.

(see My Chapter: "The Middle Coming") Mark Mallet.com/blog/the-middle-coming

"Again, I've [Mark Mallet] written in detail about this battle between the woman and the dragon over the past four centuries in my book – The Final Confrontation and in other places here.

However the dragon who attempts to devour the child, fails. She gave birth to a son, a male child, destined to rule all the nations with an iron rod. Her child was caught up to God in his throne (Rev 12: 5)

THIS IS A NEW START FOR HUMANITY

After The Destruction, A New Era Of Peace Begins We Are In the Time Of the Greatest Purification - that Is - the Destruction Of Most Of Humanity.

But This is A New Start For Humanity Like Noah And His Family After The Flood.

And It Is Not Just A New Start For Mankind - But Humans Are Being Given The Participation In The Divine Nature Of God That We Lost!

We Are Being Recreated In The Image And Likeness Of God The Way Adam And Eve Lost In The Fall.

This Is Our Birthright And Our Heritage That We

Lost And Is Being Given Back To Us If We Are Attentive And Faithful To What God Is Doing!

This Is The Biblically Promised Middle Coming Of Jesus Into Our Hearts And Souls.

[The Writings Of The Divine Will Are God's Instruction Book On How To Enter Into Living In the Divine Will – And Satan Has No Power Over *Those* Living In the Divine Will.]

This Is A New Start For Humanity!

The Divine Will Is Our Refuge And We Are Being Recreated And Sanctified To Live In The Era Of Peace.

God's Plan Is All Coming Together in Our Day! The Demons Began Their Reign On Earth Precisely When Adam And Eve Pulled Their Human Will Out Of The Gift Of Living In The Divine Will.

This is When the demons could infiltrate into the human nature and the human condition.

But as The Divine Will Is Reclaiming humans, Satan's Power Is Broken.

And the demons Are Chained And Vanquished For 1,000 Years In The Process.

WHAT IT MEANS TO DO ACTS IN THE DIVINE WILL

Book Of Heaven – Volume 17- September 17, 1924 "… Do you see what it means to do acts in my Will? This is to live in my Will: the Sun of my Will, transforming the human will into Sun, acts in it as if in Its Own Center." [The Center Of The Trinity.] "Afterwards, my sweet Jesus gathered all the books written by me on His Divine Will; He united them together, then He pressed them to His Heart, and with unspeakable tenderness, added: I bless these writings from the heart. I bless every word; I bless the effects and the value they contain. These writings are part of Myself."

His Plan

In the Following Passages, Jesus Tells Luisa His Plan To Recreate And Transform Humanity:

It The Human Will That Has Been In Charge Of Our Lives,
And God Is Using Those Living In The Divine Will To Conquer The Human Will Acting On Its Own!

Living In The Divine Will Is The Crucifixion Of The Human Will Operating On Its Own

We Sacrifice Our Own Human Will To The Divine Will And God Rushes In And Strips Us Of Everything That Is Not The Explicit Will Of God

Jesus On The Cross Is The Picture Of The Human Will Dying To Self, And Then Being Resurrected In Jesus

"As Creatures Become more Perverse, God Prepares the New Era Of The "Fiat Voluntas Tua." "This Will Complete The Work that Poured Forth from Me."

"Otherwise, The Work Of Creation As Well As Redemption Would Remain Incomplete."

Book Of Heaven – February 8, 1921
While the world wants to cast Jesus away from face of the earth, He is preparing an Era of Love: the Era of His Third Fiat.
Then he [Jesus] added: "Ah! my daughter, the creature rages more and more in evil! How many machinations of ruin they are preparing. They will reach the point of exhausting evil itself. But while they are occupied with following their own way, I will be occupied with making the Fiat Voluntas Tuus have its completion and fulfillment and My Will reign upon the earth, but in a completely new way. I will be occupied with preparing the era of The Third Fiat in which my love will show off in a

marvelous and unheard-of way. Ah! Yes, I want to confound man completely in love."

The Three Fiats

Book Of Heaven January 24, 1921

Jesus To Luisa: My daughter, The First Fiat was uttered in the Creation without *the* participation of any creature. I chose My Mother for the fulfillment of The Second Fiat. Now to achieve its fulfillment, I wish to utter The Third Fiat. This Fiat will Complete The Glory And The Honour of The Fiat Of Creation and Represents The Complete Fruition Of The Fruits of The Fiat Of Redemption. These Three Fiats will reflect The Sacrosanct Trinity on Earth, and then I will have The Fiat Voluntas Tua (Thy Will Be Done On Earth As It Is In Heaven.) These Three Fiats will be inseparable. One shall be the life of the other; They shall be one and three, yet different from one another. My Love So Desires It and My Glory Demands It. Having sent forth from The Bosom of My Creative Power The First Two Fiats, I wish to admit The

Third Fiat, since I Cannot Contain My Love Any Longer. This Will Complete The Work that Poured Forth from Me. Otherwise, The Work Of Creation As Well As Redemption Would Remain Incomplete."

New And Higher Life

The Gift Of The Divine Will Is A New And Higher Way To Live – This Is The Divine Life *That* Is The Life Of God In Heaven. (This Divine Life Is Not "New" In That Adam And Eve Lived In It Before Their Original Sin - And FALL From Grace – Jesus And Mary Lived In It, And Luisa Was Given It Back For Her And For All Humanity Who Will Receive It And Live In It.) (In The Fall Of Adam and Eve- Our First Parents-This Is Precisely When The Demons Infiltrated Into The Human Will And By This Means – Took Up Their Reign On Earth- By Influencing Humans-)

A New Heart I Will Give You

Then will I sprinkle clean water upon you, and ye

shall be clean: from all your filthiness, and from all your idols, will I cleanse you. A new heart also will I give you, and a new spirit will I put within you: and I will take away the stony heart out of your flesh, and I will give you an heart of flesh. And I will put my spirit within you, and cause you to walk in my statutes, and ye shall keep my judgments, and do them. And ye shall dwell in the land that I gave to your fathers; and ye shall be my people, and I shall be your God. Ezekiel 36: 22-28 KJV

The Heart Of God
"The Heartbeat Of My Will."

Now We Are Entering Into The Center Of The Life Of The Trinity – WHERE THE HEART OF GOD BEATS– AND LIVES IN THOSE LIVING IN THE DIVINE WILL.
God's Will Forms And Keeps All Heartbeats In Existence – But There Is Another Higher Divine Level Of God's Will Now Available To Humans On Earth,

Where The Divine Will Forms "The Heartbeat Of My Will" In Every Heart.

Who Would Turn Down The Divine Heart Of God To Beat In The Beating Of Our Heart? This Divine Will Is The Actual Heart Of God, That He Is Giving Us Right Now On Earth, (That Is, In All People Who Will Learn About It, Receive It And Live It.)

(Jesus Said That If This Divine Way Of Living Can Be Considered "New", It's Because This Way Of Living Is "New" To People Now Living.)

Book Of Heaven–

Volume 17– October 6, 1924

How the Divine Will is in the Creature like the Heartbeat in the Center of the Soul.

Luisa Speaking:

"I was fusing myself and the Holy Divine Will, and My Sweet Jesus, moving in My Interior, told me: "My daughter, how beautiful it is to see a soul fusing herself in My Will!

As she fuses herself in it, the created heartbeat takes its place in life in the Uncreated Heartbeat, and forms a single one, running and beating together with the Uncreated Heartbeat. This is the greatest happiness of the human heart: to palpitate in the Eternal Heartbeat Of Its Creator. My will makes it fly, and the human heartbeat flings itself into the center of its Creator."

"Then I said to him: tell me, my love, how many times does your will go around through all creatures? And Jesus: "My daughter, in each heartbeat of creature my Will forms Its complete round through all of Creation.

And just as the heartbeat in the creature is continuous, and if the heartbeat ceases life ceases, in order to give Divine Life to all creatures, My

Will, more than heartbeat, goes around and forms the Heartbeat of My Will in every heart.

See then how My Will is in every creature, as primary heartbeat because her own is secondary: and if I feel any heartbeat of creature, it is by virtue of the heartbeat of my Will.

Even more, my Will forms in her two heartbeats: one for the human heart, as life of the body, and one for the soul, as heartbeat and life of the soul."

But do you want to know what this heartbeat of my Will does in the creature?
If she thinks, my will runs and circulates like blood in the veins of the soul, and gives her The Divine Thought that she may put aside the human thought and give place to the word of the Will. If she works, if she walks, if she loves, my Will wants the place of her work, of her step, of her love.... **In Sum, in everything, My Will has Its Life, and with its Power, it forms the Act it Wants.**

So it maintains harmony in all created things informs in them the different effects, colors, offices of which each of them contains. Therefore, I recommend that you never go out of my will, if you do not want to multiply my sorrow, and lose the purpose for which you were created. This Gift Is Divine Life

A New And Higher Divine Way To Live

The Gift Of The Divine Will Is A New And Higher Divine Way To Live –

This Is The Gift That Adam And Eve Lost Which Has Been Given Back To Humanity-

The New Garden Of Eden Is Now Being Formed In Human Beings,

Which Will Result And Be Manifested In The Big Event- Of The Era Of Peace That All Humanity Has Been Waiting For

–All Our Human History That Is, Since Adam And Eve, Our First Parents.

We Have All Been Waiting For God To Give Us The Biblically Promised - New Hearts – And The Fullness Of The Holy Spirit- To Usher In The Promised Millennium Of Peace - The Glorious New Era For All Mankind.

All Of Human History Has Been Pointing To God Reclaiming The Earth And Mankind - With

Safeguards So That We Cannot Enter In And Try And Steal This Gift – Like Lucifer And The Fallen Angels Tried To Steal Their Angelic Grace To Do Their Own Will.

The Human Will Operating On Its Own Is The Only Problem That Exists Between God And Mankind- And Is The Great Evil-

The Breach Between God And Mankind Is Being Healed In The Gift Of Living In The Divine Will.

The Crux Of Our Life
The Greatest Treasure Is Before Us, Right Now, Called The Gift Of Living In The Divine Will.

Will We Learn About, Sign Ourselves Over, And Live In The Divine Will?

Who Would Have The Heart To Turn Down The Hearts Of Jesus And Mary?

Book Of Heaven – Volume 17- September 17, 1924

"... Do you see what it means to do acts in my Will?

This is to live in my Will: the Sun of my Will, transforming the human will into Sun, acts in it as if in Its Own Center."

(The Center Of The Trinity)

Afterwards, my sweet Jesus gathered all the books written by me on His Divine Will; He united them together, then He pressed them to His Heart, and with unspeakable tenderness, added:

I bless these writings from the heart. I bless every word; I bless the effects and the value they contain. These writings are part of Myself."

DIVINE WILL PRAYERS

Divine Will Prayer Book

A Compilation of Prayers and Meditation, Reprinted from the 1983 version. Center for the Divine Will, PO Box 5, Ortega Station, Jacksonville FL 3 2210,

Reprinted July 1996 Luisa The Servant of God, Luisa Piccarreta, who was to become known as the Little Daughter of the Divine Will, was born in Corato, Italy, province of Bari, on April 23rd 1865, and died there on March 4th, 1947, after a life which could be called 'extraordinary and the extraordinary.'

Luisa's mission in life would be to herald this Kingdom of Our Father's Will upon the earth and make it known. ...

Invocations to the Divine Will In All Our Actions

I am nothing; God is All.

Father, I love You; Come Divine Will:

- to think in my mind.

- to circulate in my blood.

- to look with my eyes.

- to listen in my ears.

- to speak in my voice.

- to breathe in my breathing.

- to breathe and my breathing.

- to beat in my heart.

- to move in my motion.

- to suffer in my suffering;

And may my soul, consumed and fused with your Will, be the living crucifix immolated for the Glory of the Father.

-to pray in me, and then offer this prayer to Yourself as mine to satisfy for the prayers of all, and to give to the Father the Glory that all creatures should give Him.

- to infuse in me the faith of Mary most holy in order to possess You as She possessed You.

- to infuse in me the hope of Mary most holy in order to desire You as She desired You.

- to infuse in me the charity of Mary most holy in order to love You as She loved You.

- to adore in me.

And since your Will multiplies acts to the infinite, thus I intend to give you the satisfaction as if all had assisted at Holy Mass, and give to all the fruit of the Sacrifice, and impetrate salvation for all."

In Other Things

"In washing: Father, I love You; come Divine Will to wash in my washing, and wash my soul of every stain.

In dressing: Father, I love You: come Divine Will in my dressing, and dress me with your Light.

In taking food: Father, I love You; come Divine Will to live in me, and nourish me with your food.

In walking: Father, I love You; come Divine Will to walk in my steps, to go in search of all creatures and call them to You.

In writing: Father, I love You; come Divine Will in my writing, and write your law in my soul.

Upon going to bed: Father, I love You; come Divine Will to rest in my rest, and extend your rest over all creatures.

To our Guardian Angel: My Angel, my Guardian, make me always live in the Will of God."

AN OVERFLOW OF HIS MERCY

The Sun Of My Will [Biography of] Luisa Piccarreta By Maria Rosaria Del Genio Published By The Vatican, Copyright 2015- Dicastero per la Communicazione- Libreria Editrice Vaticana

"It will serve for making the world know that it had to illuminate the Sun of My Will, to build His Kingdom."

From [Luisa's] "Notebook of Childhood Memories"
Pp. 219-221

"...One can well understand that this "Living in the Divine Will" is a life that brings people much closer to the life of the Blessed in Heaven.

It is the expression of that "On Earth As It Is In Heaven" of The Our Father that is so dear to Luisa." ... "Living in the Divine Will of Jesus" is the

Greatest Gift" that He wants to give people. It is an "overflow" of his mercy,

Here Is what clearly appears: this "Living in the Divine Will of Jesus" is the Greatest Gift" that He wants to give people.

It is an "overflow" of his mercy, because It is His Nature to want "to splurge even more in pouring out His love."
Love beckons love. *Realizing that Jesus has given them everything and that He has no other Gift greater than the Possession of His Will to give in order to be Loved, people will be able to cherish "the Great Good they possess" and love Him with it.*

Clearly this reciprocity looks very much like the Heavenly Love between the Divine Persons in the Most Holy Trinity!

In other words, Luisa Piccarreta tells us that remaining in The Divine Will means adhering to it completely without leaving any gaps." [It Is Continuous]

Wanting Only To Love Jesus.

From The Divine Will Prayerbook:

In every moment, in every hour, I want to always love You with all my heart.

In all the breaths of my life, breathing, I shall love You. In all the heartbeats of my heart, love, love, shall I shout. In all the movements of my body, only love shall I embrace.

Only on love do I want to speak. Only love do I want to see. Only love do I want to hear. Always on love do I want to think. Only on love do I want to burn.

Only of love do I want to be consumed. Only love do I want to taste. Only with love do I want to be content. Only by love do I want to live. And in love do I want to die.

In all instants, in all hours I want to call everyone to love. Only and always with Jesus and in Jesus will I always live. In my heart shall I sing and together with Jesus and with his Heart, love, love shall I love You.

Oh, my Jesus, You are love. You are all love. And love I want. Love I desire. Love I long for. Love, I supplicate and beseech You for love. Love invites me. Love is my life. Love enraptures my heart unto the bosom of my Lord. Of love am I inebriated. Of love am I delighted. I only, only and only for You! You only, and only for me!

Now that we are alone, let us speak of love." For pity's sake, make me understand how much You love me, because only in your Heart does one understand love.

Jesus: "Do you want me to speak to You of love?

Listen, My beloved child, My Life is of Love.

If I breathe, I love you. If my heart beats, my heartbeat tells you, love, love. I am madly in love with you. All of Creation says love to you. If the stars twinkle, love they tell you. If the sun rises, it covers you with the gold of love. If it shines with all its light in its midday fullness, rays of love does it send to your heart. If the sun sets, it is saying to you: Jesus dies for love of you.

In thunder and lightning, I send you love. And hot kisses do I give your Heart. Upon the wings of the winds, it is love that runs. If the waters murmur, I extend you my arms. If the leaves move, I press you to my heart. If the flower smells, I amuse you with love. All of creation and mute speech says to your Heart: From you I want only life of Love. Love I want; Love I desire. Love I beg from inside of my heart. I am only content if you give Me Love.

(Vol 10: 9/28/1910; 2/8/1911)

About the Author

David Sobnosky

About The Author: A Personal Note:

As My Twilight Is Upon Me,

And Our Civilization Is Falling Down Around Us,

I Hold Onto My One, But Divine Consolation,

And Make A Deep Dive Into The Pearl Of Great Price –

The Gift Of Living In The Divine Will For Which I Am Exceedingly Grateful.

And I Am Filled With That Realization That God Is Surprising Us Upon The Earth Once Again.

I Am Not A Theologian. I Have Studied This Background On My Own, And The Divine Will Has Become My Life.

BA from YSU With Majors Political Science, History And Languages.   I Do Not Claim Any Special Knowledge Of The Divine Will, But I Have Spent Countless Hours Of Watching And Listening To Recordings and Videos On The Divine Will; First in Cassette Tapes And Then Videos and Now in You Tube Videos, And The Writings Themselves.

This is Nothing Of Me, And You Can Check And Recheck If What I Am Telling You Is Correct.

The Author, A Lifelong Catholic, Studied The Bible And The Catholic Saints And The Divine Will And Wrote The Book Titled: Don't Miss The Resurrection, Published On LuLu.com in 2007, and I Have Been Studying The Divine Will Ever Since.

In My Book Don't Miss the Resurrection I Attempted To Place The Divine Will In Its Context As The Capstone Of The Catholic Church and The Capstone Of The History Of Mankind.

You Can Follow God's Revelation To Mankind In The Bible, Church History, And God's Revelation To The Catholic Saints Right Up To God Giving The Gift Of The Divine Will To Luisa Piccarreta (1865-1947) for HER AND ALL MANKIND.

The Divine Will & The Era Of Peace

God's Refuge For Our Time – Easily Explained

Author David J. Sobnosky

LIVING IN THE DIVINE WILL

God's Greatest Gift

New Book Edition

Professionally Formatted Edition

David J. Sobnosky

www.ingramcontent.com/pod-product-compliance
Lightning Source LLC
Chambersburg PA
CBHW051131300726
48978CB00011B/232